ONE FOR THE MONEY

ONE FOR THE
MONEY

DICK BELSKY

Published in 1986 by
Academy Chicago Publishers
425 North Michigan Avenue
Chicago, IL 60611

Copyright © 1985 by Dick Belsky

"Two More Bottles of Wine"
Words and Music by Delbert McClinton
© Copyright 1975 by Duchess Music Corporation
Rights Administered by MCA Music,
A Division of MCA Inc., New York, NY
Used by permission

Printed and bound in the USA

No part of this book may be reproduced
in any form without the express written
permission of the publisher.

Library of Congress Cataloging-in-Publication Data

Belsky, Dick.
    One for the money.

    I. Title.
PS3552.E533805   1985   813'.54   85-18545
ISBN 0-89733-221-0

Chapter 1

The first time I heard of Nancy Kimberly was on a sweltering July afternoon.

I was at my desk at the *New York Blade*, the newspaper I write for, when the news of the murder came over the police wire. The *Blade* offices are located downtown in a big old building on South Street, next to the East River. From where I sit in the city room, if you crane your neck a bit, you can see about a half mile along the river, giving you a panoramic view of much of the borough of Brooklyn and both the Brooklyn and Manhattan bridges. Some days I crane my neck a lot.

It was a Friday, a bit past one o'clock, and the temperature in New York City had hit 102. Outside, the East River Drive was already filling up with cars on their way to Fire Island or the Hamptons for the weekend. Traffic was jammed, and the drivers looked hot and frazzled. Alongside the highway, water from the river broke gently against wooden piers. Sailboats drifted by.

I was just thinking about how nice it would be to be on one of them, sailing north out of the harbor and on up the New England coast, when my telephone rang.

"Lucy Shannon," I said.

"Lucy? This is Walter Barlow."

Walter Barlow is the city editor of the *Blade*. At the moment he was sitting at his desk, about fifty feet away from me. For some reason, he hates to talk to reporters face-to-face. So instead of calling you to the city desk or coming over to you, he rings you on your extension. No one knows why, but he's been doing it for sixteen years. I didn't like him.

"Hi," I said breathlessly, "we've got to stop meeting like this."

"I need someone to go out on an assignment," he said. "What are you doing right now?"

I looked over the stuff on my desk. There was a half-worked Jumble Words from that morning's *Daily News*, the remains of a roast beef special from the *Blade* cafeteria, a press release from a Councilman detailing his achievements of the past six months, a press release from the American Automobile Club announcing that this was National Auto Safety Week, a letter from a woman in Queens who said she was in contact with men from Venus, a note from the office personnel department asking if I wanted to sign up for more life insurance and an advertisement from a tire company reminding me that it wasn't too early to start thinking about buying snow tires. That was it. There was nothing from Deep Throat telling me to meet him in an underground garage for new exclusives on Watergate. Jackie Onassis hadn't called to offer me a personal interview. No mass murderers wanted to give themselves up to me today. It was beginning to look as if I was going to have to wait at least another day for my Pulitzer.

"I'm free," I said.

"Good." He began to read from a piece of paper that had moved on the police wire next to his desk. "At about 1300 hours this afternoon officers were called to investigate a report of a death in an apartment building in the 19th Precinct. Two patrol cars responded. When they arrived, the building superintendent directed them to one of the apartments where the body was. The victim was a female and it's been ruled a homicide. The perpetrator has not yet been apprehended.' Are you getting all this?"

"Look, Walter," I said, "twenty people are murdered in New York City every day. Most of them don't make the paper and a lot of them even the police don't care about. Now do you have any plans to tell me what's so special about this one, or are you going to keep it to yourself as a scoop until after deadline?"

"The people in the police shack tell me she's an attractive young woman in her early twenties," he said, after a short pause. "She's from Teaneck, New Jersey, which could mean some money. She came here to become an actress or a model and she lived in a luxury building on the Upper East Side. She must have been paying at least a thousand a month."

Now I was interested.

"What's the address?"
"Three eighty-nine East 78th."
"Name?"
"A tentative ID – Nancy Kimberly. Police have not been able to notify the next of kin yet."
"Anything else?"
"I think that's all. Police are still on the scene. Oh, and please remember that you've only got a couple of hours until deadline. I want to hear from you no later than four o'clock. Now don't forget."
"Walter, I'm thirty-three years old. I've been a reporter here for ten years. I'm not a copygirl. I know what the goddamn deadlines are."

He hung up before I could slam the phone down on him.

On my way out, I passed the city desk. Barlow wasn't there, but Annie Klein was. She was an assistant city editor.

"Hi Lucy," she said. "Did I just hear you and my boss going at it again?"

"No, no. You're mistaken. I was just suggesting to him that he watch Lou Grant reruns more often. He needs to brush up his gruff but warm-hearted city editor image."

She laughed. "He's not that bad," she said. "Just a little strange."

"He's a complete idiot," I said. I looked down at her desk. She was working on a staff assignment schedule.

"Do you know what to put me down for?"

"No," she said. "You got a biggie?"

I shrugged. "Someone named Nancy Kimberly

got herself killed on the Upper East Side. I'm going to check it out now."

She wrote it down next to my name. "How about tomorrow?" she asked. "Do you have an assignment yet?"

"You're gonna love this one. They want me to do an interview with the President of the City Council, looking back on what's been accomplished in his first year in office."

"B-o-o-o-ring," she said.

"You know me. I just do what I'm told."

"Yeah. Listen, maybe this murder will run into tomorrow, and you can get out of the other thing."

"Nope," I said as I headed for the elevator. "These kind of murders are all alike. I'll have this story wrapped up before I go home tonight. It'll be a big splash in the papers for a day or so, and then – unless they catch the guy who did it – it'll be the last time any of us ever hear of Nancy Kimberly."

I was dead wrong, of course, but how could I know that then?

Chapter 2

I walked out of the *Blade* and into the steambath outside. The temperature was now up to 103. By the time I got to the subway station at the Brooklyn Bridge stop, about four blocks away, the back of my blouse was soaked with perspiration. I got on the IRT headed north. There was no air conditioning.

As murders go, this sounded like a pretty good one. The victim was probably attractive. A career girl. Upper East Side. It was the kind of thing that pushes all those boring stories about Ronald Reagan and disarmament talks off the front page and back to page 58, next to the crossword puzzle.

The high-rise, on the north side of 78th Street off Second Avenue, was a white-brick building with a grocery store and a dry cleaners on the ground floor. Across the street was a restaurant that looked like a singles hangout: a lot of guys in Pierre Cardin suits and girls dressed like Diane Keaton were eating lunch at tables covered with checkered cloths. A sign was fastened to the white bricks:

"Luxury apartments. Owner management. 24-hour security. Inquire within."

I wanted to inquire within, but there looked to be a problem. Two cops were standing guard by the door to make sure no one got in who wasn't supposed to. I was pretty sure that included me, so I sat down on the curb in front of the restaurant for a while and thought about it.

I didn't see any other reporters around but I knew that much of the free world's press was going to arrive in about five minutes. If I was going to get the jump on them, I would have to do something in a hurry. I knew one ploy, but I had never used it myself. A police reporter on another paper had told me he passed himself off as a cop at crime scenes. He would say "I'm Doyle from downtown," in a loud, official voice, and barge in. He said it almost always worked. Now that there were a lot of women on the police force, I thought maybe I could get away with it too.

One cop was a sergeant but the other one looked like a rookie. While I was standing there trying to get up some courage, the older one wandered off inside the building.

I took a deep breath and made my move.

"I'm Shannon from downtown," I said brusquely.

The kid hesitated. I didn't know whether he was going to ask for my credentials or whether he wasn't used to women cops yet.

"Listen," I said. "I've got a lot of work to do up there. I don't know whether you know it, but

One for the Money 9

there's a murderer running loose. Are you going to direct me to the scene of the crime, or are you just out working on your suntan?"

"No, ma'am, I'm sorry, ma'am," he said. "It's on the seventh floor, apartment 7E. Lieutenant Masters is up there already."

The door to 7E was open. Inside a lot of police types were standing around a short, stocky middle-aged guy who seemed to be the super. He wore a green work outfit, a soiled baseball cap and had a tattoo on his right arm. He didn't look happy.

What was left of Nancy Kimberly lay in the center of the living room in a pool of blood. It looked like she had been stabbed over and over. All her clothes were stripped off, and she had been badly beaten. Her face was grotesque, a mass of blood and black and blue flesh that made it hard to believe she could once have been a pretty girl. Her blue eyes gazed vacantly at the ceiling.

"I've already told you everything I know," the guy in the green suit was saying. "Somebody called me about an hour ago. They said they heard a lot of screaming coming from this apartment. I didn't think much of it, but I came up to quiet them down. I knocked, there was no answer. I tried it a few more times, then I decided just to open up the door, you know, look in to make sure everything was all right."

He pointed to the body.

"That was what I saw."

The lieutenant named Masters took out a stick of gum, unwrapped it slowly and put it in his mouth.

He chewed thoughtfully for a second.

"How well did you know her?" he asked.

"How well do I know anyone in this building? This is New York. There's 330 apartments here, and the turnover you wouldn't believe. She moved in about a month ago. I think the only times I saw her was when she looked at the apartment to rent it and then about two days ago when she had a leaky faucet."

"What did she seem like to you?" Masters asked.

The man shrugged.

"She was pretty. Someone said she wanted to be an actress. That's all I know about her."

"And those two times were the only two times you were with her?"

"Yeah, that's all."

"You're sure now?"

"Yeah."

Masters stared at him intently.

"Hey, wait a minute," the guy yelped. "You don't think I had anything to do with this, do you? I told you. I only seen the girl twice in my whole life."

"Maybe you did and maybe you didn't," said Masters. "Maybe you came up here to work in the apartment and noticed she was a pretty young thing. Maybe you came back and made a pass at her. Maybe she didn't like that. One thing could've led to another, and you hit her. Then you hit her again. Then you were afraid she'd talk about what had happened, so you picked up a knife and did a job on her. Is that the way it happened?"

"No, no, no," the guy screamed. He looked

scared, but he didn't have to be. I could tell Masters didn't believe any of that himself. His heart wasn't in it. He was just trying it on for size. He let the subject drop and began talking with a couple of cops nearby. I wandered over to another part of the room.

There was a small desk against a wall near the window. Quietly, I went through the drawers. At first I didn't find much, just junk mail, bills and cancelled checks. The only thing I learned about Nancy Kimberly was that she didn't pay her bills on time. There were a lot of overdue notices. Finally, I came across a packet of pictures. A dazzling girl with auburn hair and classical features smiled at the camera. On the back of each shot there was a biography of Nancy Kimberly—what jobs she'd had, her age, her interests, etc. Publicity stills. I slipped a few into my purse.

I looked further. There was a birthday card from her parents. She had turned twenty-three last month. "Dear Nancy," the card said, "may this year be filled with good blessings and may you find happiness in whatever you do. We love you. Mom and Dad."

There was also a paycheck for $102 from Stereo Heaven on W. 10th Street in the Village. And a handwritten note on plain white stationery from someone named John. It said, "Nancy, we've got to discuss this. We can't simply ignore it and hope it will go away." That ought to be easy to track down, I thought. All I have to do is talk to everyone named John in New York City. My sleuthing didn't turn up much else. No confession notes. No bloodstained fingerprints. The killer hadn't left behind any maps showing how to get to his house.

I wandered over closer to the body. Doing my best not to attract attention, I wrote down a description of the apartment – the size of the living room, the color of the walls, that sort of stuff. Then I walked over to the body and took what notes I could. It took a superhuman effort not to get sick. Lying next to the body was a bloody kitchen carving knife. I wrote that down too.

I was heading to check out the rest of the apartment when I got caught.

"Hey," someone yelled, "who the hell is she?"

I stopped in my tracks and looked back. They were all staring at me: Masters, a detective sergeant standing next to him, about six other cops, the guys from the medical examiner's office and the super in the green suit. Suddenly, Masters groaned. "Oh, no, it's that goddamn Shannon broad from the *Blade*. Jesus Christ."

"Hi there," I said brightly.

"What's she doing here?" the sergeant asked.

"I'll tell you what she's doing here," Masters yelled. "She's here because she's a goddamn nosy, smartmouthed bitch."

"Hi there," I said.

I was going to have to come up with something new to say pretty soon.

Masters turned to the sergeant. "Higgins, get her out of here. Get her out of my sight."

"Hey, wait a minute," I said. "Now that I'm here, how about a few questions? You're going to have to

One for the Money 13

talk to the press sooner or later anyway. Just tell me what you know so far."

"We don't know anything," Masters said.

"What about the cause of death?"

"We don't know anything about that either."

"Well, look," I said. "It seems obvious that she was beaten badly and she was stabbed. Those seem to be the two most likely causes of death. Is there anything else that might have killed her?"

"We're not ruling anything out at this point."

"Nothing at all is ruled out?" I asked incredulously.

"Nothing at all," he said.

"How about old age?"

He let that one pass.

"What about the knife?" I asked.

"What knife?"

"The knife with the blood all over it lying next to the body."

"Oh, that knife. What about it?"

"I figured maybe it was a clue," I said. "But then, what do I know? I'm not a sophisticated crime fighter like you boys."

Masters turned to the sergeant again.

"Higgins, I want you to escort Miss Shannon personally down to the street. And if she gives you the least bit of trouble, I want you to arrest her and throw her in the can overnight."

The sergeant took my arm and walked me out of the apartment. I didn't resist. Higgins seemed somewhat amused by the whole business. I had already checked him out. He wasn't Robert Redford, but he wasn't bad. He had wavy blonde hair and bright blue eyes. He was big, over six feet, with broad shoulders. I figured him to be in his middle thirties, maybe a little older than me.

"That was a cute trick you pulled getting in here like that," he said. He had a nice smile.

I shrugged. "It's something I always wanted to try," I said. "You know how it is."

"I guess I do. But it didn't help your relationship with the Lieutenant any. You two don't get along too well, do you?"

"We've only met on a few stories," I said.

We reached the bank of elevators.

"Okay," he said, pressing the button. "Now please don't try to sneak back in, or I might end up walking a beat in the South Bronx. You wouldn't want that to happen to me, would you?"

"I sure wouldn't," I said.

I tried to think of something else to say, but my mind was a blank. Christ, I was coming on like Debbie Boone.

The elevator doors opened.

"Well, see you," he said.

"Yeah," I said. He would never forget my one-liners.

The doors started to close; he held them back with one hand.

"Listen, Lucy Shannon," he said. "I'm really interested in the tricks of your trade. If I called you up and offered to ply you with liquor and a free dinner some night, could I get you to divulge some of them?"

"Sure," I said wittily. "No problem. I'm in the Manhattan book."

How about that? Who says a woman starts to lose her sex appeal after thirty? I wasn't getting older, I was getting better.

"Hey," I yelled after him down the hall. "If you want, you can tell Masters I got tough with you and you had to work me over with a blackjack. That'll make his day."

Then the elevator doors closed, and I rode down. A crowd of reporters was gathered outside the building. I tried three pay phones before I found one at 73rd Street that worked.

"Barlow here."

"Hello, sweetheart," I said, "get me rewrite."

He put me on with Tom Egan, the paper's best rewriteman. I gave him everything—the super's explanation of how he found the body, the description of the room, the biography stuff on Nancy Kimberly—all of it.

"Wow, that's pretty good stuff," he said. "The wires and the radio have almost nothing. How'd you get all this?"

"Diligence and clean living," I said. "Listen, I also have a publicity picture of her. If you send a copyboy up here right now, you'll have it in time for the first edition."

The copyboy showed up about twenty minutes later. I gave him one of my copies of the picture and then made a sweep of the stores in the neighborhood to see if anybody remembered the girl. A few of them recognized the picture and gave me a few quotes about brief encounters with her. I called this stuff in too.

By the time I got back to the office, it was close to

ten o'clock. The story in the first edition took up most of page one. "Actress, 23, Slain on East Side."

They used the picture of the girl very big on page one. The story ran for several columns and jumped to page three. There was a picture of the exterior of the apartment house. It was pretty impressive.

By the time I made a few adds and corrections to the copy for the late editions, the office was nearly deserted. After all, it was Friday night in the Big Apple. I might go to Studio 54 and hang out with Halston and Liza Minnelli. Or maybe I'd go to Elaine's and let Woody Allen buy me dinner. Or maybe I'd win a million dollars in the lottery.

I took the subway home, stopping off at 14th Street to buy a pizza. I ate it in bed, watched a rerun of *The Honeymooners* and fell asleep a little after midnight.

Chapter 3

I was living in a high-rise on East 18th Street, just off Gramercy Park. My apartment cost nine hundred a month, about twice what I could afford. It was tiny and cramped, the walls were like paper, cockroaches had taken over the kitchen and the super had the hots for me. I called it home.

A ringing sound in my ear woke me up. I reached over and clicked off my alarm clock. Nothing happened. The ringing kept going. I tried picking up the phone by my bed. If that didn't work, I was going to have to do something drastic, like getting up and seeing if it was the doorbell.

"Hi, Lucy, rise and shine. This is Annie at the city desk. Forget about that council assignment. We want you to do a follow on the Nancy Kimberly murder."

"What happened? Anything new?"

"We've got an address for her parents in New Jersey: 5511 River Road in Teaneck. It's an unlisted phone number, so I'd like you to drive up there today. No one else has any quotes from the parents yet."

"Okay," I said. "What time is it?"

"Eight-thirty."

I groaned. "Jeez, what are you doing to me? Listen, I can't get going for a little while. I've got some things I have to do."

"Like what?"

"Like running to the bank, dropping off some cleaning."

"This is still a daily paper we're putting out here, you know. We've got these things called deadlines, you ever hear of them?"

"I need this stuff for the weekend, Annie. How about sending a copyboy over to take care of it for me? It would really help. Then I can run right up to Teaneck now."

"I can't do that."

"Why not? Annie, you want this story, don't you?"

She sighed. "Okay, I'll send a kid over. What do you want him to do?"

"Just have him talk to my doorman. I'll leave the instructions with him. He'll tell him where the bank is and the cleaners and everything."

"Are you sure you don't want him to do anything else while he's there?" she said. "Like maybe do your grocery shopping or mop your kitchen floor?"

"Well, now that you mention it. . ."

She hung up on me.

I took a long, hot shower, put on my robe and slippers and padded to the front door to pick up the morning papers. Then I brewed some coffee and scrambled three eggs in a frying pan. I ate breakfast in the living room while I went over the papers. None of the competition had anywhere near the details my story had.

Feeling good, I took the dishes into the kitchen and rinsed them off. I took a long time brushing my hair. Then I slipped into a gauzy brown sleeveless loose top with a full matching skirt and rummaged through my closet for a pair of two-inch beige sandals. I picked up my Sony tape recorder, threw my notebook into my big straw handbag and checked myself out in the mirror. I looked good. Lucy Shannon, big time New York City media star. Eat your heart out, Jane Pauley.

I left instructions for the copyboy with the doorman and then I made it all the way down to the garage to get my car without anyone asking me for my autograph. In fact, no one asked me anything, except the garage attendant. He wanted to know when I was going to pay my bill. I told him it was in the mail.

I left the garage and picked up the East River Drive, heading north, at 23rd Street. It was a nice day. The sun was bright and the weather bureau was predicting another scorcher but it was still early enough to be comfortable. A gentle breeze was blowing off the East River. I figured the drive to Teaneck would take about thirty minutes.

I turned on WHN, the country music station. All the good rock stations are on FM and the radio in my 1971 Volkswagen only had AM. So on the road

I was a country music freak. That year my favorite was a song by Emmy Lou Harris called "Two More Bottles of Wine". It went like this:

> The way he left sure turned my head around
> Seemed like overnight he just up and put me down.
> Ain't gonna let it bother me today
> I been workin' and I'm too tired anyway.
> But it's alright 'cause it's midnight
> And I got two more bottles of wine.

I thought about what I had to do when I got to Teaneck. Questioning the relatives of murder victims is never pleasant. The key, I told myself, was to do it tastefully. Be considerate of the family's feelings. Compassion at all costs. Knock, knock – *New York Blade* calling. Hello, Mrs. Kimberly, sorry to bother you at a time like this, but our readers want to know how you felt when you heard some sex maniac had killed your daughter with a butcher knife.

I thought about what else I could do to earn a living. Maybe I should answer one of those ads on matchbooks and get into hotel administration. Or reply to one of those TV spots that say you too can earn big money in the field of air-conditioning repair. Hell, what was I making fun of those people for? At least they didn't routinely invade people's privacy and spy on their most anguished moments.

I crossed over the George Washington Bridge into Jersey, slowing down a little to admire the New York skyline to the south, and then picked up Route 4 into Teaneck.

Teaneck is not superexclusive like Rye in Westchester or the Hill in Englewood, but it supplies your basic comfortable suburban existence. Nice houses, lots of trees, green grass, no crime. The Kimberlys' house was a two-story red brick on a pleasant street within sight of the Hackensack River, about a half mile from the Fairleigh Dickenson campus. I parked my heap in the empty driveway and walked up the wide front steps. Across the street two teenaged boys were tossing a baseball back and forth to each other. A power mower was running somewhere nearby. It was only fifteen miles from New York City, but it seemed like about a million.

I rang the doorbell. There was no answer. After a few minutes, I wandered around the house and tried the back door. No answer there either. I peered in a back window and rapped loudly on it. Nothing. I came back out to the front and tried the same thing at the living room window. Still nothing. No sound inside the house.

Trained reporter that I am, I was beginning to suspect that no one was home.

"Looking for someone?"

I turned around. A middle-aged man was walking toward me from the house next door.

"I'm trying to find the Kimberlys," I said.

"Not home."

"Yeah, I was getting that impression. Do you have any idea where they are or when they might get back?"

"They went away," he said.

"I think we've established that."

"No, I mean they went away—away on a trip. Some kind of round-the-world tour. They left two weeks ago. They won't be back until sometime next month."

He eyed me closely. In fact, he seemed to be leering at me.

"This is about the girl's murder, huh?" he asked. "There was another reporter here earlier from one of the TV stations asking for them. I told him the same thing I told you. You're a reporter too, right?"

I acknowledged that I was.

"Say, if you want to ask me some questions, why don't you come over to my place? We'll get in out of the hot sun, sit down, have a beer and talk. I got lots of time. The wife's away."

He winked. He was definitely leering now. The neighborhood lecher, I thought to myself. The kind of guy who works in the city as a bigshot lawyer or Wall Street broker, then comes home to Jersey and hangs out near schools and Brownie meetings with a bag of candy.

"Sure," I said, flashing a smile, "that sounds like a swell idea."

Who says I won't do anything for a story?

We walked across his yard, went in through the back door and sat down at the kitchen table. The remains of his breakfast were still there, and the sink was full of dishes. I wondered where his wife had gone. Wherever it was had to be an improvement.

"I'm Charlie Allen," he said, sticking his hand out.

I shook it. "Pleased to meet you, Charlie. Lucy

Shannon. I work for the *Blade*."

"Want a beer?"

I nodded.

He brought over two cans of Budweiser, put them on the table in front of us and pulled his chair closer to me.

"So what is it you need to know?"

"Tell me about Nancy Kimberly. What kind of a person was she? How long did you know her? Anything you can remember would be helpful." I opened the flip top and took a swig of beer. "I'm not trying to pry or anything like that. We just want to give people some idea of what she was like. I think that's what her parents would want if they were here."

"She was a bitch," he said.

"I beg your pardon?"

"A bitch. A real bitch. She really thought she was something. Little Miss Movie Star, that's what she thought she was going to be. Well, I noticed that after she moved to New York, she didn't exactly set the show business world on its ear, did she?"

"Let me take a wild guess," I said. "You didn't like her."

"You're damn right I didn't. I don't like stuck-up broads."

He took a big gulp of beer and belched loudly. I wasn't quite sure about the correct response, here. Should I excuse him? Should I belch back? Should I just ignore it? I opted for ignoring it. But I made a mental note to check it out in Emily Post when I got back to the office.

"She used to sit out in the backyard there

wearing a flimsy bathing suit." He pointed out the window toward the Kimberlys' back porch. "The bitch knew every man around was staring at her. That includes me, I don't deny it. Hell, I'm only human. But then after sitting out there like that for all the world to see, the goddamn tease acted shocked if anyone noticed her. I tried to talk to her a few times. Just being friendly, you know what I mean? But she went running to her parents claiming. . ." His voice trailed off. "Well, she made up some stories to her parents," he said.

I nodded uneasily. This conversation didn't seem to be getting me anywhere.

"What exactly happened to her again?" he asked.

I told him.

"Jeez, that's an awful way to go, isn't it?" He stared at his beer can.

"When's the last time you saw her?" I asked after a while.

"Oh, I don't know. Maybe a few months ago. She hasn't lived here for a year or so. I heard she went to live in the city to try to break into show business."

"Did she have any close friends that you know of?"

"She used to come home sometimes with this guy who looked like a fairy. I heard he was her boyfriend."

"A fairy?"

"You know—long hair, pretty boy clothes. A real creep."

"Do you know what his name was?"

"The only thing I know is once or twice I heard her call him John."

I remembered the note in her desk. It was from someone named John.

"Any other friends you can remember?"

"Well, there's the Feinsteins a few houses down this street. They've got a girl, Susan, the same age as her. Susan and Nancy were friends in high school."

"Maybe I can find out some more from them," I said. I finished my beer and put the can back on the table. "Thanks a lot for the beer and all your help."

He wanted me to stay longer, but I made an excuse about deadlines and beat a hasty retreat. Outside on the sidewalk, I looked back and saw him watching me from his window. Okay, I thought, that was a real waste of time. Now what?

The mailbox on the house two doors down said "Feinstein". I rang the bell, and a woman opened the door. She was heavyset, about fifty with silver-grey hair. She was wearing a red-patterned housecoat and her eyes were red too, as if she'd been crying.

"Mrs. Feinstein? My name is Lucy Shannon of the *Blade*." I showed her my press card. "I'm sorry to bother you, but someone said your daughter was a friend of the Kimberlys down the street. I wondered if I could talk to you or your daughter for a few minutes about Nancy Kimberly."

She slammed the door in my face.

I may not have many positive qualities, but I am persistent. I leaned on the doorbell for a few minutes. She opened the door a second time.

"Will you please go away?"

"No," I replied.

"Don't you people have any decency at all? We're in mourning here. Leave us alone."

"All I want to do is ask..."

"A young girl is dead," she screamed.

"It doesn't do any good to yell at me, Mrs. Feinstein," I said quietly. "I didn't kill her."

She stared at me.

"Look," I said. "I know it's a hard time for you, but I have to try to find out more about Nancy Kimberly. It's my job. So I can either stand outside your house here until you're ready to talk about her, or you can invite me in now. In all honesty, Mrs. Feinstein, I'd rather come in now and get it over with. It's awfully hot out here."

She smiled slightly.

"Yes, I imagine it is, Miss Shannon. Oh, all right, come on in then."

I followed her into the living room. It was a spacious, homey-looking room; its windows faced out onto the Hackensack River. We sat down on the sofa. On a coffee table in front of us was a picture of a girl about Nancy Kimberly's age. I assumed it was Susan Feinstein. Next to the picture lay the morning's papers, all of them open to the story about the murder. One of the stories was mine.

"You seem to be very good at your job," she said. She picked up a cup of coffee from the table and took a sip. She didn't offer me any. I guess this was to let me know I wouldn't be staying long. "This

One for the Money

barging in on people grieving over a death—is it something you do often in your line of work?"

"Too often," I said.

She nodded. Her mood seemed to have softened a bit.

"Is your daughter here?" I asked.

"No, she's away at college. She's working on a master's degree at the University of Michigan."

"Were your daughter and Nancy close friends?"

Mrs Feinstein looked sadly over at a large box sitting on the floor. She got it and put it down in front of me.

"That should answer your question," she said. "I was just going through it when you came."

The box contained picture after picture of Nancy growing up with Mrs. Feinstein's daughter—playing in the backyard, in her prom dress, going off to college. There were letters to the Feinsteins from camp or while she was away on vacation. There was even an essay from Nancy's eighth grade English class: "What I Want To Be When I Grow Up: An Actress."

"Susan and Nancy were inseparable through grade school and high school, they were like sisters. Wherever one went, the other wasn't far away. We used to kid them about it. Nancy spent so much time over here I used to say I was going to start charging her rent."

Mrs. Feinstein closed her eyes for a second and her face contorted. Then suddenly she started talking. I'd seen the same thing happen a few times before with grieving people. They are totally uncooperative at first and then something opens up inside and you can't shut them up. It's a kind of emotional release, I guess. Mrs. Feinstein went on non-stop about Nancy for more than an hour. I took notes furiously. When she was finished, I felt as if I had known Nancy for years.

I was just about to ask her if I could borrow some of the stuff from the box when the telephone rang in another room.

"Excuse me," she said.

After she left I thought about it for a few seconds. Then I began stuffing some things from the box into my purse. I thought to myself as I did it what a swell person I was. This was the second day in a row I had swiped some personal things of Nancy Kimberly's. I was really getting good at it. Anyone have any memories or treasured mementos of a loved one? Better keep them locked up if Shannon's around. She's not really a bad girl, that Shannon. But she'll do anything for a story.

Mrs. Feinstein came back into the living room.

"Just a call from a friend who'd heard about the news," she said in a strangled voice.

I nodded and looked at my watch. It was well into the afternoon. I had to get back soon and write my story for the Sunday edition.

"Just one more question before I go," I said. "You talked a lot about how Nancy and your daughter were such good friends in grade school and high school. What about recently? Did they still see each other?"

Mrs. Feinstein heaved a sigh.

"I don't know quite how to put this, Miss Shannon, but Nancy changed in the past few years. She was always a bit wild and sometimes—if Susan wasn't around—she ran with a bad crowd. But when she went away to college, she changed. She wasn't the same girl when she got back. We still loved her, please don't misunderstand."

"How did she get along with her parents?"

"Oh, well, they think—thought the sun rose and set on Nancy. She was their only child. They're away, you know, on a round-the-world tour. No one knows how to contact them. I just don't know what's going to happen when they hear about this awful thing."

"You said she was wild, Mrs. Feinstein. What exactly did you mean?"

"Well, I don't want to overstate anything. But... when I heard what had happened to Nancy, I was terribly upset... but over these past few years I've had this feeling... I thought she was heading for trouble. I guess she was the kind of girl things happen to. Bad things. But of course I didn't expect... not this bad..."

"Did you ever meet a boyfriend of hers called John?"

"John Luckman. Yes, she brought him over here a couple of times. He seemed all right. It was none of my business. She was old enough to make her own decisions."

"Do you know where I could find him?"

"No. I think he ran some kind of store in the Village."

"Stereo Heaven on West 10th?"

"I'm sorry. I really have no idea."

She sat on the couch staring at her daughter's photograph. "I haven't told Susan yet," she said. "I keep going over to the phone. But I can't make myself do it."

The house was silent except for the whirring of an air conditioner. I couldn't think of anything else to say and it was getting late. So I thanked her and let myself out.

Chapter 4

On Sunday morning, after I picked up the papers from outside my door I hurled the Sunday *Blade* across the living room.

They had used my story, all right, and it was dynamite. It was played big across the top of page one, with a huge jump inside and lots of the pictures and excerpts from the letters I had taken from Mrs. Feinstein. The streamer headline read: "The Girl Who Wanted To Be a Star". And underneath: "Exclusive report by the Blade's Lucy Shannon."

But someone had changed my lead. I had led off with a quote from Nancy's eighth grade essay about wanting to be an actress, and had dropped quotes from the essay throughout the story. I thought it gave a really dramatic effect. The new lead said simply: "Friends and relatives in Teaneck were shocked today over the slaying of 23-year-old Nancy Kimberly in her New York City apartment." It was a lead first used around the time of John

Peter Zenger and repeated approximately 12,672 times since then. A real hack job.

I stewed about it all day, but I wasn't sure if I should make a scene. The next morning when I got to work Barlow made up my mind for me. On my desk, I found a note from him saying that I was to stay inside the office all week and work on rewrite.

I walked over to the city desk. Annie and some of the others nearby saw the look on my face and tried hard to look busy.

"Walter, I want to ask you a question."

Barlow looked up from the copy he was reading. He seemed uncomfortable. Maybe I should go back to my desk and phone him on the extension, I thought. "Yes, what is it?" he asked finally.

"Have you ever considered taking up a career in journalism?" I said.

Someone snickered.

Barlow's face turned red. "What exactly is your problem today?" he said.

"Well, for openers, there's this note that I'm on rewrite all week. Why am I being taken off the Kimberly story?"

"The Kimberly story is over," he said. "It's had its run. You did a couple of pretty good stories, and that's the end of it. You can't make a career out of it. The other papers have already dropped it. This is a big city, we have to move on to other things."

"Trust me, Walter," I said. "I have a feeling about this case. I know there's a story in it that hasn't come out yet. I want to follow up a couple of things today. For instance, there's the stereo store in the Village where Nancy Kimberly worked..."

"You're on rewrite, Shannon, and that's the end of it. Any other questions?"

"Yeah. Did you rewrite my story?"

"That's right. I did it," he said.

"Why? What was your reason?"

"I did it because I'm the city editor, and I thought it made better sense that way. I didn't understand your lead."

"Did you read the whole story? It was explained down further in the piece, you know."

"I didn't finish reading it. I was busy with other things. But I read the lead, I didn't understand it and I changed it. That's my job here."

"Do me a favor," I said. "The next time you want to rewrite a story of mine, read it first, okay?"

He didn't answer. I guess he didn't want a blowup in front of whole office. But I was sore and I didn't care who knew it.

"I know reading a long story all the way through is tough for you," I said. "After awhile your lips must get tired."

Barlow exploded.

"Who the hell do you think you are?" He was shouting and everyone in the office was looking. "I don't have to sit here and take that kind of crap from you. You're nothing. What makes you think you're such an expert on newspapers? What have you ever done? You're no Carl Woodward, you know."

"Bob," I said.

"What?"

"It's Bob. Bob Woodward. Bob Woodward and Carl Bernstein. They were reporters for the *Washington Post* who wrote a series of stories that forced a president to resign. It was called Watergate. Maybe you heard about it. It was in all the papers."

He swiveled around in his chair to let me know the conversation was over.

I walked back to my desk and sat down. Tom Egan next to me was checking out the murders that had moved on the police wire overnight. You had to check them all out, even the ones in the crummiest parts of town, just in case some night a woman killed in a brawl at a South Bronx social club turned out to be Brooke Shields or somebody. It was part of the routine.

"Hello, Sarge," he said into the phone. "This is Egan at the *Blade*. This stiff you found in an abandoned building in Harlem last night, do you have an ID yet? You do. So tell me, is this guy going to be any loss to society?"

Egan listened for a minute, then wrote down "drug addict" next to the item on his list. He moved to the next one and dialed the number of another police station.

"Lieutenant, this is Egan from the *Blade*. About the body you found in Bedford Stuyvesant last night, the one with the numbers slips in his pocket. Who was he—a noted brain surgeon or what?"

Maybe Barlow was right, I thought to myself. There were a lot of murders going on every day. Why was I getting so excited about one of them? It was just that I had this feeling about Nancy Kimberly that I couldn't shake.

I knew what I was going to do. It was a bad move on my part, I was sure, but some things you just have to take a shot at and see what happens.

Picking up my bag with the tape recorder in it, I began walking across the city room toward the elevator. Barlow looked up at me.

"Where are you going?" he asked.

"I'm going to work on the Kimberly story," I shouted back over my shoulder.

"Get back on rewrite. I'm the editor here, and I'm telling you you're not going."

"Screw you," I said and kept on walking.

I took the F train to the Village and walked along 10th Street until I found Stereo Heaven. It was a small store located between a bookshop and a pizza parlor. The front window was covered with pictures of Billy Joel, Men at Work and Michael Jackson. When I pushed the front door open, a bell tinkled.

There were several teenagers clustered around the front of the shop. One of them was asking for the latest Boy George album. No taste, I thought. There was only one clerk on duty at the checkout counter. She was a plumpish blonde girl who looked to be in her early twenties. She was wearing corduroy levis and a tight T-shirt with "Stereo Heaven" printed across the front of it. I browsed in the rock section and found an old Band record I had been looking for and took it to the counter.

"Hi," I said. "Is John around?"

"John Luckman? He's not here today. I'm expecting him any time. You want to wait? Or I could give him a message."

I decided honesty was the best policy.

I told her who I was. "I want to talk to him about Nancy Kimberly," I said. "And what's your name?"

"I'm Karen Tunney. Yeah, isn't that awful about Nancy? She worked here off and on. She was John's girlfriend. She had a lot going on in her life. She was trying to break into show business and modeling so she only worked here when she was desperate for bread."

She had to excuse herself for a minute to wait on the teenagers. They were buying a Prince record. While she took the money they danced to the music that was blaring through the store. I thought of my friends and me buying Beatle records twenty years before. I thought someone should tell these kids they had awful taste in music, but I didn't want to be the one.

When they left Karen Tunney began to wrap my records. We made some small talk. She asked me if I liked The Band and I said yes. She asked me if I had seen *The Last Waltz* and I said I had. She asked me whether I thought Robbie Robertson was dreamy and I said he was. She asked me what I liked to listen to and I said the Stones, Springsteen and the old Byrds. She asked me if I was into Dylan and I told her I was. She said she could dig where I was coming from.

Now that we were fast friends, I returned to my theme.

"Do you remember the last time you saw Nancy?"

"Oh, quite a while ago. I don't remember exactly.... Maybe five weeks ago? I remember they had a big fight that day."

"Who? Nancy and John? Do you remember what they were fighting about?"

"Oh, they didn't need a reason to fight. She's a Sagittarius."

"She's what?"

"She's—she was a Sagittarius. That's her sign. He's a Taurus. That's a bad combination, causes lots of conflict. Are you into astrology at all?"

"Well, I read Jeanne Dixon sometimes to see if I'm going to meet a tall handsome stranger later in the day."

"Oh. Anyway those two were a volatile mix. Cosmic, if you know what I mean."

"Do you remember anything in particular about that last day? Anything you can think of might be helpful, you never know."

"Well, I do know it was a crazy day. Because we were having a sale on a whole bunch of new releases —The Police, Joan Jett, like that—and the place was really packed all day. You could hardly move in here. Once two kids started fighting and we had to call the cops. And then later there was this whole mix-up with a woman who left a briefcase here. Just a real crazy day."

"I don't quite get the part about the woman and the briefcase."

"This woman just came in to buy a record. She

put this briefcase on the counter to get the money out of her purse and I guess she forgot it when she left. Janet noticed it afterward. Janet Langmann. She's another girl who works here. So anyway the woman's name and address and phone number were on a card in a little pocket on the outside of the briefcase so Janet gave it to John so John could get in touch with the woman. We thought she'd come back when she noticed she'd left it, but she didn't."

"And that's all that happened?"

"Well, actually I think they had a fight about that."

"John and Nancy?"

"Yeah, I think that was what they were fighting about. They got into this big fight after Janet gave him the briefcase. And then John acted kind of funny about it."

"How do you mean, funny?"

"Well... I asked him later on that afternoon if he'd been able to locate that woman who left the case. I was just making conversation, you know? I mean, what did I really care about it? So he blew his top at me. He told me to mind my own business and forget about the briefcase and just worry about the work I was being paid to do. He said I'd be sorry if I didn't. It was a heavy scene." She dropped her voice. "It kind of scared me. He never talked to me that way before. I didn't expect it. I knew he could be a mean guy sometimes..."

"Mean enough to kill somebody?"

"I didn't say that. He couldn't have killed Nancy.

Are you kidding? He loved her. I mean, people have fights, it doesn't mean... She was a very loveable girl to men."

She flipped the little tab back and forth on the bag with my records in it.

"Do you think that business with the briefcase meant anything?" she said. "Maybe there was something valuable in it, huh?"

"I don't know. It's a very confusing case."

"Yeah." She handed me the bag. "Hey," she said, "are you into biorhythms at all? We've got some great charts here. Maybe they'll help you find some clues."

I said thanks, but I had to be moving along. If things didn't clear up soon, I might take her up on it.

"You've been a big help. One more thing. Do you know where John Luckman lives? I'd like to talk to him."

"Don't tell him I told you," she said.

"I promise."

"It's an apartment a few blocks from here on 12th Street." She gave me the address. "And listen, like I said, be careful about what you say to him. He's not the nicest guy in the world."

"Don't worry about me," I said. "I'll be careful."

There was a coffee shop down the street from the record store. It was getting close to lunch time so I found a seat at the counter and ordered a hamburger and a coke. While I was eating, I thought about John Luckman. He sounded like a real sweetheart. Obviously he needed a crash course from Dale Carnegie.

My scenario for the case went something like this: Luckman came over to Nancy Kimberly's apartment. They argued. Maybe the argument was about something valuable in that missing briefcase or maybe it was over something more mundane like the way she cooked broccoli. Anyway, he killed her in a fit of rage. Once he started, he didn't stop until he had mutilated her. Then he fled. I thought about it some more. I sort of liked it. In fact, the more I thought about it, the more I liked it. It had a nice, orderly ring to it.

The problem was how to deal with this guy Luckman. If he really was the killer and he found out I was onto him, he might smash my head in too. I tried to decide what my plan of action should be. I finally decided I didn't have one. I'd just have to wing it and see what happened. After paying my bill, I went back outside and walked up to 12th Street.

Luckman's apartment was in an eight-story building near the corner of Sixth Avenue. The directory in the lobby said he lived in Apartment 5H. There was no doorman. I pushed the button for the fifth floor. The elevator door was just opening when I heard someone coming through the front door behind me. It turned out to be my old friend, Lt. Masters and two of his men from the Homicide Squad. Higgins, the sergeant I had the hots for, wasn't one of them.

Masters saw me and groaned.

"Oh, this is wonderful," he said. "It just makes my day seeing you again, Shannon. What in hell are you doing here?"

I smiled demurely.

"Okay, how did you find out about this guy?" he asked. "We just got on to him an hour or so ago ourselves."

"I heard about him a couple days ago," I said. "I've just now gotten around to stopping by. Jeez, you guys are really on top of this case, aren't you?"

We stared at each other for about thirty seconds.

"So you gonna tell me how you found out about him or not?" he asked.

"Ever vigilant, that's our motto in the Fourth Estate," I said.

One of the cops standing next to Masters snorted. "C'mon," he said. "Let's go on up and get this over with."

The elevator doors opened again, and the three of them stepped in. I got in too.

"Where do you think you're going?" Masters asked.

"It's a free country," I said. "I was here first. I'm going up to see him too."

"Oh, for chrissakes, let her come," one of the cops said. "Maybe that'll shut her up."

Masters nodded. "Okay, but you wait outside until we're finished. Understand?"

We rode up the elevator in silence. Apartment 5H was at the end of the hall. When we got there, Masters rang the bell. There was no answer. He rang it a few more times and then knocked on the door. When he did that, the door opened by itself. Someone hadn't bothered to close it all the way.

"Let's take a look," Masters said.

"Isn't this called breaking and entering?" I asked.

Masters looked at me wearily. "Shannon. Give it a rest."

They went in, followed closely by me. Nobody tried to stop me. Luckman's apartment was pleasant, nothing special. An L-shaped living room, with sunlight streaming in through a wide undraped window. The furniture was simple Scandinavian—a sofa, an easy chair, a glass coffee table, some shelves filled with books, TV, stereo. A kitchenette to the left of the front door. It looked like a thousand New York apartments.

The bedroom was down the hall. The door was open, and that's where we found John Luckman. He was lying on top of the bedspread, wearing a sweat shirt, torn jeans and a pair of sneakers. We registered that, but it wasn't important. What was important was the large red splotch in his forehead. The blood had dried, but it had seeped down the pillow and stained the bedding. Luckman wouldn't have to worry about the cleaning bill. His eyes were open, just as Nancy Kimberly's had been, and he was just as dead as she was.

Chapter 5

The news of this second murder hit the front pages of the New York papers like World War III. The murder of a pretty girl on the East Side was spicy enough. Put that together with the murder of her boy-friend in an apartment on the other side of town, and you have the sort of thing that makes newspaper circulation soar.

Not that there wasn't plenty of other news around that July. The President was in China for talks. New York hovered on the edge of fiscal disaster again. The Yankees were fighting for a pennant. And the city was in its second week of a torrid heat wave; every day Con Edison issued frantic warnings that sounded as though the next person who plugged in an electric toaster stood a good chance of blowing out the entire Northeast power grid. But the only things people were really talking about were the Nancy Kimberly murders.

The whole thing had made me a sort of celebrity. I had written three exclusive stories on the case.

And I was actually there when the second body was discovered. Channels 2, 5 and 7 all interviewed me on the air, I answered questions on a radio call-in show and Bill Beggs left a message for me asking if I wanted to be on a panel show later in the week discussing how the media in New York covers crime. I was very hot.

On Tuesday morning, the day after the Luckman murder and with my story plastered all over the front page of the *Blade*, I walked triumphantly back into the city room. Barlow did not look at me. There was a note on my desk from Dan Hodges, the managing editor, saying he wanted to see me right away.

Hodges was a middle-aged, balding man who had been at the *Blade* for over twenty years. He had done everything at the paper—working his way up from copyboy to reporter to city editor and finally to managing editor. He was a good newspaperman.

"You said you wanted to see me," I said. "No doubt to tell me about a big raise on the way?"

"First of all," he said, "I want to say that your stuff on the Kimberly case has been outstanding. The best stuff you've ever done. We've been on top of this story from day one, and we're beating the hell out of the other papers. It's a nice feeling."

"It's nothing any superstar journalist couldn't do," I said.

"Second of all," he continued, "I called you in here to tell you that if you ever again directly disobey an order from an editor at this paper, I'll fire your ass out of here so fast you won't know what hit you."

"Now, wait a minute, Dan..."

"No, you wait a minute. Okay, between you and me, I know Barlow isn't the world's greatest city editor. But he's your city editor, and as long as he's here, you have to do what he says. You can't run a newspaper any other way."

"Dan, he's an idiot. Do you know what he wanted me to do?"

"I don't care. That's not the point."

"Well, I think it is. I knew what had to be done, and I did it. And I was right. You can't deny that."

"Listen, Lucy, do you think you're the only person around here with problems like this? You should see some of the idiotic things the publisher wants me to do. But he's my boss, so I do them."

"Well, there's a difference between my situation and yours," I said.

"What's that?"

"You go along with that shit. I don't."

Hodges took off his glasses and rubbed his eyes.

"You always have to make everything hard, don't you, Shannon?"

"Dan, this is a super story, and I'm not letting up on it. Either I cover it my way for this paper, or I cover it for someone else."

"Just simmer down. No one's taking you off the story. Not now, anyway. We couldn't if we wanted to. But as long as you're here you have to take orders from Barlow. Is that understood?"

I didn't answer.

He smiled at me. "Of course, that doesn't mean you have to take orders silently. I would never try to curb freedom of speech in a newspaper city room."

I smiled back. "Okay. I'll try to be good."

"Now get out there and get some more exclusives on this thing. *The Blade's* been selling like hotcakes since Friday. I want it to keep selling."

Out in the city room, I walked up to Barlow's desk. He was going over some copy.

"Hi chief," I said. "Got anything for me?"

He didn't look up.

"Because if you haven't, I think I'll head over to Homicide. Check out my sources and all that. See you around."

The Homicide Squad office that was handling the case was on East 67th Street, in the 19th precinct offices. A cop at the door gave me a visitor's pass and directions. I trudged up to the second floor.

The Squad office was a small room. Needless to say, it was not air conditioned. The windows were open and a big fan whirred noisily from a corner. A few cops sat at desks, but Higgins wasn't there, and neither was Masters. I went up to a desk with a nameplate that said Sgt. John LoCicero, introduced myself and asked for Higgins.

LoCicero was dark and balding. His shirt sleeves were rolled up and his collar was open. "He'll be in later," he said. "He's working the night shift this week. Eleven to seven."

"And Masters?"

One for the Money 47

"He's out on a case. Is there anything I can help you with?"

"I was wondering about the Kimberly case. Any developments since yesterday?"

"Oh, yeah, right. Shannon. I thought I recognized the name."

He tipped back in his chair, wiped his forehead with a folded handkerchief, and told me that ballistics tests indicated Luckman had been shot with a .38 caliber pistol. He had been dead since Friday, the same day Nancy Kimberly had been killed. Time of death could not be fixed any more precisely than that.

"There were some fingerprints in the room, they're being tracked down now. But they could turn out to be Luckman's or his girl friend's. We're not too hopeful about that. And we don't have a motive. Two murders, and it's a little early for a solution."

On my way out I noticed a typed list attached to the wall near the door. It was a staff list of Homicide cops and their addresses and phone numbers. Sgt Edward Higgins lived in Manhattan, on the West Side.

I asked one of the cops if I could use a phone, and dialed Higgins' number at an empty desk. He picked it up on the third ring.

"Hi," I said. "I'm a citizen. I need police assistance."

"What?"

"Maybe you remember me. Lucy Shannon? You threw me out of a building last week."

"Oh," he said, "that Lucy Shannon. What kind of assistance did you have in mind?"

"Well, I think I may be in very grave danger of having to eat dinner alone tonight. So I thought if you're not busy we could stake out a restaurant or something."

"That might fit my schedule. It might even be fun."

"I thought so. And educational too. We could exchange ideas on modern police technology and the importance of a free press. Then you could show me how your handcuffs work and I'll explain the inner workings of a great newspaper. And if we get bored with that, maybe I'll let you frisk me. So what do you think?"

"Unfortunately tonight's out. I'm tied up for a while and I have to be at work by eleven. But tomorrow night would work."

"Terrific. I get off work about eight. That'll give us a few hours anyway. Do you want to come to the *Blade* or meet me somewhere?"

"I'll pick you up."

I gave him the address and we said goodbye. I picked up a telephone book from the desk and leafed through it to see if there was a listing for Janet Langmann, the other girl who worked at Stereo Heaven. There was a Janet Langmann listed on East 80th Street.

The phone was picked up on the first ring.

"Is this the Janet Langmann who works at Stereo Heaven?" I said.

There was a pause.

"Hello?" I said.

"This is her mother," the voice said. It sounded kind of funny. "What do you want her for? Are you a friend of hers?"

"No," I said. "I just wanted to ask her something."

"She's not here," the woman said. Her voice faded out a little. "I don't know where she is."

"Is something wrong?" I asked. I realized suddenly that she was crying. "Listen," I said, "my name is Lucy Shannon. I'm a reporter for the *Blade*. You can talk to me. What's wrong?"

"I'm so worried about her," the voice said.

"I'll be up there in five minutes," I said. "Just hang on."

I grabbed a cab. Cold chills were travelling up and down my spine.

Janet's mother was a small woman, fiftyish, with dark hair set in a bouffant style. She was wearing a sleeveless cotton dress and holding a ball of tissues in her hand. Her eyes, behind large black-rimmed glasses, were red.

"I don't know what to say to you," she said.

We settled down on a bright red futon sofa. It was a cute studio apartment, with unframed posters on the walls.

"Would you like something to drink?" she said, and burst into tears again. "I'm just so worried," she said. "She never showed up for dinner Saturday, and she didn't call or anything. That's not like her. And she didn't answer the phone. That's why I came over here today; the super let me in. I don't have a key. I never thought I'd need one. I mean, why would I..."

"Lots of young women go away for a few days, Mrs Langmann," I said. "I'm sure you have no reason to worry. She probably just took a long weekend somewhere and she's too busy to call."

"I know my daughter. She never goes anywhere, even overnight, without telling me about it. And last Saturday was her sister's birthday. She wouldn't forget that. She'd have been there... if..."

She began to weep again.

"I don't know what to do," she said.

In the pit of my stomach I had this awful feeling that she had a reason to worry.

"You'd better call the police," I said.

When the cops got there, Mrs Langmann told them about her daughter, and I filled them in on Janet's link to Nancy Kimberly. The cops looked worried. Obviously this wasn't just another missing person report. Mrs Langmann got really upset.

When I finally got back to the city room it was about 6:30. Most of the staff were finishing their stories for tomorrow's paper.

"Hey star," Annie Klein yelled, "did you find another body today?"

I really didn't think that was funny.

"Maybe," I said. "A girl is missing. She's connected to the Kimberly case so she could be dead. I've been with her mother."

"Jesus Christ," Annie said.

I had just started writing the story when Barlow

and Dan Hodges came over to me.

"What's this about another dead woman in the Kimberly case?" Hodge asked.

"Not dead," I said. "Or anyway right now just missing. Her name is Janet Langmann. She worked in that record store with Nancy and Luckman. Her sister had a birthday party on Saturday and Janet didn't show up. No one's heard from her since. I just left her apartment."

Barlow snorted. "Big deal," he said. "She's probably out somewhere getting laid."

"Dan," I said, "something's wrong. I'm afraid she may be dead."

Barlow shook his head. "All you've got is a girl who didn't call home for a few days. There isn't enough there for a story."

"Dan," I screamed.

"Okay, okay," Hodges said. "Walter, I'm going to overrule you on this. We've been ahead on this story all the way because of Shannon and I'm going with her on this. If the girl turns up and she was just having a little fling we'll look silly. I grant you that. But I'm willing to take the chance. The cops are treating this as a missing persons case, right?"

"They're very worried about it, Dan," I said.

"Okay, go ahead and write it."

The piece was my fourth Page One Blockbuster in five days. The headline read: Kimberly Pal Missing: Police Fear Third Death. We ran a huge picture of Janet Langmann that her mother had given me, and a smaller one of the record store taken from across the street. The caption called it a "death store", and asked: "Who's killing the people of Stereo Heaven?" The whole package took up virtually the entire front page.

God, I thought, the other papers were going to shit when they saw this in the morning.

I waited until the first papers came off the presses a little after midnight, so I could take a couple copies home with me. I drove my usual route home: South Street to East River Drive, then north all the way to the 23rd Street exit. I was on the Drive when I first noticed a brown Lincoln keeping several car lengths behind me. It stayed with me all the way.

I pulled into my garage, and took the basement elevator up to my apartment on the sixth floor. I locked the door behind me and went over to the window. I looked down at the street through the slats of the blinds. The brown Lincoln was parked in front of the building.

Inside a trunk in the back of one of the closets was a .45 caliber handgun. I had brought it back with me from Vietnam in the early '70's when I was over there writing about the war. I had never used it but I always felt safer knowing it was there, just in case I woke up some night and found a motorcycle gang in my bedroom.

Now I dug it out from the bottom of the trunk, loaded it and set it on the table next to my bed. Then I sat in bed, propped up on two pillows, hardly moving a muscle, for what seemed like several hours.

During that time, absolutely nothing happened.

No one took any shots at me. No one tried to kidnap me. No one put any live tarantulas in my bed. Maybe I was being hysterical, I told myself. But I knew I wasn't.

I was just starting to doze off when the phone rang. I looked at the clock next to my bed. It was 1:50 a.m. I didn't know anyone who would be calling me at 1:50 a.m.

"Hello," I said cautiously into the receiver.

The voice on the other end was muffled. If you want to go on living, Shannon, forget about Nancy Kimberly."

That was all. Then just a click and after a while a dial tone.

I got up and walked around for a few minutes. I was very aware of being alone. No husband for protection. No children. Not even a dog. I poured myself a double Scotch on the rocks. My hands were trembling, the ice clinked against the side of the glass. I looked out the window. The brown Lincoln was gone. But I stayed awake the rest of the night with the .45 next to me.

Chapter 6

Higgins picked me up at the office the next night about eight o'clock. I looked up from the paper I was reading and there he was, walking toward me across the city room. Strong, purposeful strides. Clear blue eyes. He was wearing an open-necked white shirt, grey slacks and a blue checkered sport coat. It's too bad I have to work later, I thought. I'd like to invite him up to my place after dinner to see my etchings.

The city room was nearly empty.

"Where is everyone?" he asked. "I expected to find Clark Gable yelling 'Stop the presses!' and Cary Grant telling them to rip out the front page."

"They all go home at 6:30 now," I said. "Everyone's in the union."

Higgins shook his head. "That's disappointing."

We went down to his car. "The whole paper's put out during the day now," I said, "and especially in the late afternoon. The first edition comes off the presses about 6:30. And after that all we do is make a few changes and updates. The whole business has changed."

"No more yelling? No more colorful characters? Not *The Front Page*?"

"It's professional. It's corporate. Most papers now are run by Wharton School graduates. They talk a lot about demographics, circulation growth areas, profit margins... you know, romantic things."

We went uptown to the Abbey, a restaurant in the East 20s where I eat often. "It's Irish, huh?" he said.

I ordered a Scotch and soda and he got a light beer.

"Okay," he said, "say something funny."

"Who do you think you're having dinner with— Henny Youngman? Anyway, I'm not in a funny mood. I'm still thinking about how the romance went out of journalism."

"You wanted to be Rosalind Russell in *His Girl Friday*," Higgins said, "and it hasn't worked out."

"You know what my all-time favorite newspaper movie is?" I said. "*Deadline USA* with Humphrey Bogart. You ever see it? Well, it's about this big metropolitan newspaper. The owners have just announced that it's shutting down the next day. The staff is working on the last edition. And they've got this story—it's hot, it could be dangerous, but it's a big story. Bogart's the editor and he hears one of the guys in the city room say he doesn't want to cover it; he doesn't want to risk his life for a paper that's closing the next day. So Bogart says to the guy, 'You're fired.'

"The guy's all upset but it's too late. So then later he asks another reporter, 'How about you? You have any objections to covering this story?' And the second guy grabs his hat. He says, 'Who, me, chief? No sir, I'm on my way.'"

I took a long drink.

"God, I love that kind of thing," I said. "I suppose I sound like a nut."

"No, no," he said. "I understand. You're the reporter who grabs his hat and covers the story, right? You're not the guy who wouldn't go?"

"Absolutely the guy who goes," I said. "The trouble is, there aren't too many editors around like Humphrey Bogart."

"What's your editor like?"

"Please," I said. "Not while I'm eating."

Actually I felt more like drinking than eating. It had been a long day, and I still hadn't gotten over that phone call last night.

"Tell me something about your life that doesn't involve newspapers," he said.

"There isn't much about my life that doesn't involve newspapers."

"Have you ever been married?"

"Jeez, I'm glad you reminded me," I said, dropping my fork. "I've got to call my husband and remind him to take the pot roast out of the oven and make sure he picked up the kids from school."

Higgins stared at me.

"Just kidding," I said. "I wanted to see if you were still paying attention."

"Be serious."

"Okay, the answer is no—I've never been married."

"How come?"

"Well, it's okay for some people, I guess. But it just wouldn't work for me."

"Oh."

"I lived with someone for a year once," I said. "He was a dentist. We lived on Long Island."

"A dentist?"

"That surprises you?"

"It just doesn't seem like the kind of guy you'd be interested in. How'd you meet him?"

"It was just one of those things. He picked me up in Central Park. It was a spring day, and I was sitting on a bench reading a paper. We started talking and he asked me to dinner that night."

"Just like that?"

"Yeah," I said. "I think he liked my teeth."

"So what happened?"

"After a while I moved in with him. We had this big house, and every day we'd commute to work together on the Long Island Railroad. In the evenings and on weekends, we'd sit on the back porch and listen to the crickets or work in the yard or do all the other things people do in the suburbs."

"But it didn't work out?"

"No. It was my fault. One morning I woke up, looked around and said to myself: 'Hey, there's nothing happening here.' So I moved back to the city, and here I am."

"Forever?"

I shrugged. "Who knows? What about you?"

"Well, I was married until about a year and half ago. We had a house in Closter, New Jersey. Now I'm divorced, and I live in the city too."

"Did you get divorced about anything in particular or was it just your basic all-around rotten marriage?"

"We fought a lot. We fought about our bills, the money I spent on the car, the color we were going to paint the house—you name it. But mostly, I guess, we fought about kids."

"You had kids?"

"No. We had no kids. That's what the fights were about. I wanted them. She didn't. So we got divorced. She moved to the West Coast, and I sold the house and moved to Manhattan. It seemed silly staying there in New Jersey all by myself."

"Do you like living in the city?"

"I hate it. I hate all the noise, the dirt, the rudeness. I want a house with a yard and fresh air and a garden. I like to sit on the porch and listen to the crickets."

"Is that all you like to do?" I asked. "I mean you can only sit around and listen to crickets for so long. What else does Ed Higgins do when he's not playing police sergeant?"

"Well, I like sports a lot."

"Which ones?"

"All of them," he said. "I've got season tickets for the Knicks, the Rangers, the Giants. Plus I go to about fifty Yanks and Mets games a year, and I've got cable TV. Sometimes I watch as many as five ball games in a night. On a good weekend—when I'm stacked up with beer and potato chips—I don't even have to leave my apartment."

"God," I said, "no wonder your wife left you."

"You don't like sports?"

"Nah, I hate 'em. They bore me silly."

I took a bite of my Dublin Grill. "We make some great matchup, huh?"

"Yeah," he said dryly. He was having Shepherd's Pie.

"How is it?" I asked. He said it was good.

"You know," he said. "I think something's going to happen in that Kimberly case."

"I think so too. But do you have any official reason to think so?"

"For the record," he said, "the police are pursuing a number of leads which we are confident will end in a quick apprehension of the criminal or criminals. Off the record, we don't know what the hell's happening."

"There's this girl who works at the record store—Karen Tunney. If someone's killing off all the people who worked there. . ."

"We offered her police protection, but she turned it down."

"That's kind of dumb," I said. "All the people around her are dropping like flies."

"She's checked with her astrologer. It's a

favorable month for her. No prospect of danger. She doesn't want someone watching her all the time."

"I suppose she hasn't got anything to hide," I said.

He drank some beer. "You can never be sure."

"You know, I was thinking about John Luckman," I said. "Is there any possibility he could have killed himself? I mean, you know, killed his girlfriend and then shot himself? It happens."

"No way. There's a lot of reasons why it couldn't have been suicide, but the main one is that no weapon was found in the room. What did he do? Shoot himself in the head point-blank and then get up and walk down the hall to the incinerator, drop the gun in, go back to the apartment. . ."

"I get it," I said. "I never claimed to be Sherlock Holmes."

"You don't have to be Sherlock Holmes to figure that out," he said.

The waitress brought Irish Coffee.

"There's a lot of funny stuff about this case though," I said.

"Like what in particular?"

"Like how Nancy Kimberly made a living. She only took home a hundred a week from the record store. And she only worked there about a month. How did she afford that apartment? Did a rich uncle die? Did she have another job that we don't know about? Did she sell Girl Scout cookies door-to-door? Something doesn't add up."

"We thought about it," he said. "Of course her

folks might have helped her out. We haven't been able to talk to them."

"Maybe she was involved in something illegal."

"Like what?"

"I don't know. Drugs... prostitution..."

He sipped his coffee. "She doesn't have a record," he said.

"The police don't always know about everything."

"God knows that's true," he said. "But give them a little credit. They may be smarter than you think."

"You like being a cop," I said, "don't you?"

"I'd better. I've been one for over ten years. How about you? You sounded a little bit disillusioned tonight. You thinking of changing careers?"

"I think about it all the time. I have this book at home—I've had it since I was in high school. It lists different occupations, alphabetically, from A to Z. Sometimes I go through it and daydream about what I could be doing. But I can't make up my mind. When I read the A's I want to be an advertising executive. When I get to D, I think I should be a doctor. And then there's L, and law school."

"What part are you reading now?"

"T. At the moment I'm torn between teacher and taxidermist."

He laughed. "How about P and policewoman? You'd make a good cop."

"I thought about it, but I didn't like those shoes. Did you ever walk a beat?"

"Of course I walked a beat," he said. "What do

you think? I walked a beat in Brooklyn for years. Bay Ridge."

"And then Homicide. Has Masters been there as long as you have?"

"No, longer. I've only been there about two and a half years. I went from Brooklyn to Narcotics. Masters is all right, don't sell him short."

When we left the Abbey I told Ed he didn't have to bother driving me home. I wanted to stop by the station anyway and see if there was anything new. We took Third Avenue uptown. Traffic was heavy. We got bogged down around 59th where a lot of movie theaters were just letting out.

"I keep thinking about Nancy Kimberly's body," I said. "The way it was hacked up. Just killing her didn't seem to be enough for whoever did it. They seemed to want to obliterate her, wipe her away. Or maybe it was a warning to others—maybe she doublecrossed someone with a nasty disposition."

"What's this guy doing in the middle of the street?" Ed said. He gave a blast on the horn.

"I know this isn't a mob style killing," I said. "I mean they didn't stuff her in a trunk or float her down the East River in a garbage can. But maybe they had an extra grudge against her, or they were interrupted..."

"Yeah, it's not mob style," he said. "I think Masters can handle it. You don't want to get yourself all tangled up with possibilities."

"Listen, Ed," I said. "Somebody followed me home last night. And I got a nasty phone call."

I told him about it.

"You need some kind of protection," he said. "Why don't I try to arrange it?"

"I don't see how I could work with an escort," I said. "And even though the whole thing made me very nervous at the time, I don't think they'll hurt a newspaper reporter."

"Have you checked your horoscope?" he asked.

We found a parking spot on East 65th Street, and walked the two blocks to the stationhouse. I amused myself watching them book a teenage junkie who had just snatched a woman's purse, while Ed went upstairs to the squad room to see what they'd found out during the day. He came back with a big smile on his face.

"There's really not much new," he said, "but there is one thing. You were right. We checked during the day and found that Nancy Kimberly had spent a bundle in the weeks before she died—expensive furniture, a new car and practically every designer dress in town."

Suddenly he leaned over and kissed me. Square on the lips. I kissed him back. Right there among all the dope addicts, flashers and muggers. It was very nice.

"Hey," I told him, "this is the first time I've ever kissed anyone in a police station."

"Me too," he said.

Chapter 7

By the time I got out of the police station it was nearly 11:30. I decided to catch a cab home. It was a five dollar ride down to Gramercy Park, but I had a better chance of getting there alive than if I rode the subway. The subway costs only 90 cents, and the Mayor maintains it's safe to ride at all hours. But then again, you never see the Mayor riding it at 11:30 at night.

I walked over to Second Avenue and tried for about fifteen minutes to hail a taxi. A half dozen passed me with off duty signs, and twice people jumped into open ones before I could get to them. One cabbie just drove past ignoring me. Maybe I looked like a mugger.

I was thinking about trudging down Second Avenue a few blocks and trying it there when a car pulled up to the curb. It was a black Cadillac with two men in the front seat. One leaned out the window and spoke to me.

"No reason to take a cab," he said. "We'll give you a ride."

Before I knew what happened, the guy was out of the car and alongside me holding onto my arm.

"It's a nice night," I said. "I think I'll walk. I like to walk."

The guy pulled back the jacket of his coat to show me a holster with a gun in it. His hand was around my arm like a vise. Just in case I didn't get the message, he made it perfectly clear for me.

"You really don't have a choice, Miss Shannon. Now get in."

I climbed into the back seat and he got in beside me. He kept his hand inside his coat, near the gun. We drove east over to the FDR, then headed south.

Both guys were right out of a B-mobster movie. Large, swarthy Italians dressed in dark suits. They were sweating a lot. The guy driving had disgustingly greasy hair that had been slicked down and combed straight back.

I decided I could either cower in fear or play it loose and casual. I don't like cowering, even in a situation like this. I decided to let them think they weren't scaring me as badly as they were.

"That's a nice hairdo," I yelled to the guy in front. "I think maybe you're overdue for an oil change, though."

No one laughed. Greasy Hair turned around and glared at me.

"Keep it up, baby," he said, "and you may not be so pretty anymore."

"Nice dialogue," I told him. "You watch a lot of old George Raft movies to get your technique down?"

One for the Money

The guy next to me snorted in disgust. "Ignore her, Les," he said. "The boss says this broad thinks she's a goddamned Joan Rivers or somebody."

Since my audience didn't seem appreciative, I decided to suspend the comedy routine. We rode in silence for awhile. Les took us all the way down the FDR to the Brooklyn Bridge, then across the river and onto the Brooklyn-Queens Expressway. We took that south and finally wound up in Bay Ridge. Bay Ridge is one of the city's Italian enclaves, the place where John Travolta was supposed to live in *Saturday Night Fever.*

"Who's the boss?" I asked.

The guy next to me smiled slightly. "Mr. Gianni," he said. "Ever hear of him?"

I'd heard of him. Anthony Two-Ton (Tony) Gianni. He was the owner of something called Gianni's Sand and Gravel Company in Brooklyn. In reality, there was no sand and there was no gravel. Gianni's business was gambling, loansharking and narcotics. He had been indicted thirteen times in the past twenty years but never spent a day in jail. I'd written about him a few times. Once I'd done an analysis of organized crime in New York in which I called him one of the most powerful and esteemed underworld bosses in the country. I hoped he remembered that.

We pulled up in front of a restaurant with a big electric sign that read: "Antonio's—Italian Foods." A kid came out and took the car.

Inside red-coated waiters hurried round carrying scrumptious-looking pastas and meat dishes. We walked through the crowded dining room. Everyone seemed to be having a good time. A few drinks, some good food, pleasant conversation. No one seemed to notice that in the middle of it all Lucy Shannon was being kidnapped.

"Help," I wanted to yell, "someone save me."

We went into a banquet room in the back of the restaurant. There was only one person eating there, a huge man at a big table. Food was piled high on several plates in front of him. Two waiters stood by nervously. No one had to tell me this was Anthony Two-Ton Gianni.

"Hello, Miss Shannon," he said pleasantly. "Thank you for coming. I hope it wasn't an inconvenient trip and that Les and Rocky were polite."

"Heavens no," I said. "It was a lovely ride. And such intellectually stimulating conversation, too. Les and I discussed the SALT II treaty, Norman Mailer and this season's schedule at the Royal Ballet Theater. We were just getting into analyzing some of Shakespeare's sonnets when we ran out of time."

"I'm truly sorry you had to be brought here in so crude a manner," he said. "Won't you sit down?"

I sat down.

"But you see," he went on, "I wanted very badly to see you. We have some business to talk about."

"What business could I possibly have with you?" I asked. "I don't owe anybody any money, I'm not in the market for heroin."

Gianni held up a huge hand. "We'll get to our

business in due time. But first—eat. What strikes your fancy? The cuisine here at Antonio's is excellent, I assure you."

"No thanks, I just ate."

"Are you sure you won't have something? Maybe a little pasta. Or an antipasto. Just to be kind to Antonio. He likes people to eat heartily at his place. No? That's a pity. Do you see this sauce?" He pointed to a dish in front of him. "It's a rare kind of pesto sauce that's made correctly only in a few restaurants in the entire Western Hemisphere. This is one of them."

He took a taste and savored it. "Hmmm, delicious," he said.

"Wonderful," I said, "but I'm not Craig Claiborne. I don't give a crap about your fucking food. Are you going to tell me why you brought me here or not?"

He put his fork down and stopped eating. The games were over. His voice became more serious.

"I thought we could exchange some information," he said.

"About what?"

"About Nancy Kimberly. You tell me what you know, and I'll tell you what I know. Does that sound fair enough?"

"You go first," I suggested.

"A short time ago," he said, "this young woman named Nancy Kimberly came into possession of something that was—ah, well, you can just say it was very important to me and my associates. For some time we didn't know where this thing was, just that we didn't have it anymore. But eventually we tracked it down to Miss Kimberly and a friend of hers, John Luckman." He took a mouthful of pasta.

"Unfortunately," he went on, "both of them are dead."

"What a pity," I said. "And you still don't have what you're looking for. So what is it you expect me to tell you?"

"Anything you know. You seem to be very much at the center of this whole thing. Whenever something happens, you're there. I think you may have come across something we overlooked."

"One thing I don't understand," I said. "Why didn't you get this information out of Nancy Kimberly and John Luckman before you killed them? Wouldn't that have been a lot easier?"

He frowned. "Kill them? I didn't kill them, Miss Shannon."

"Okay, then you had them killed. Same thing."

"You got it wrong," he said. "We don't operate that way. I didn't have anything to do with killing them."

"I don't believe you," I said.

He shrugged and ate some more sauce.

"Well, if you didn't kill them," I said, "do you know who did?"

"That's a police matter. Why not ask your friend on the force? Detective Sergeant Edward Higgins, isn't it?"

"You want me to know you're watching me. Why are you having me tailed?"

"In my business you have to take precautions. Like I said, you may know something I don't know. I like to know everything. So how about it? Come on. We had a deal, didn't we?"

"I didn't have any deal with you," I said. "If you want to find out what I know about this story, then pay thirty cents like everyone else and read it in the *Blade*."

Les was getting restless.

"Goddammit, boss," he said. "I'm tired of listening to her lip. Why are you fooling around with her? There's only one way to handle a broad like this. I'll show you."

He lunged at me, lifted me up out of my chair by my elbow and grabbed my breast hard. Then he drew his hand back and slugged me across the face. The blow landed on the side of my mouth. I could taste blood. My legs wobbled and the room was spinning, but I wouldn't give them the satisfaction of seeing me fall. I pulled away from him and grabbed hold of the table for support.

The smart thing to do here was to sit down in the chair again and be quiet so Les could cool off. But I'm famous for hardly ever doing the smart thing.

"Is that your best punch?" I said, sneering. "I've been hit harder in a pillow fight."

He came at me again. A few years earlier I had taken a course in martial arts for women. I didn't stick with it long, but I remembered our instructor telling us the best way to immobilize a man was with a surprise kick in the groin. Bend your leg at the knee, pull it back and extend it, then kick forward with all your might at the target. Bend, extend, kick. Les wasn't expecting me to fight back, so he left himself open. When he was fairly close to me, I let fly with a kick that had every ounce of strength I could muster.

It was on target all right. He let out a strangled shriek and dropped to the floor like a sack of wet cement. Gianni half-rose from his chair, still holding his napkin.

"Stop it, stop it," he shouted. "This is getting us nowhere."

I leaned against the table breathing heavily. "Now you say that. Why didn't you say that when he was winning?"

"Things have gotten out of hand," Gianni said. "All I want to do is talk to you. I'm not looking for any violence."

"No, you're not looking for any violence. Your goons grab me off the street, drive me halfway across the city, rip open my blouse, try to molest me and then slug me in the mouth. But you're not looking for any violence. Fuck you."

Les was still moaning loudly on the floor, holding his crotch.

"Can you keep it down a bit, Les?" I said, over my shoulder. "We're trying to hold a conversation here."

"I wouldn't be so flip with him," Gianni said. "Les may not be too bright, but he holds a grudge for a long time. He won't forget this."

"I'm shaking," I said.

I was still out of breath and my face hurt.

"Is the fun over?" I asked Gianni. "Can I go home now?"

"Let's just talk for a while longer," he said.

We went around and around like this for a long time, him asking me the same questions and me giving him no answers. Not that I had much I could have told him even if I wanted to. After a lot of this, we all got in the car and began driving around Brooklyn. All except Les. He didn't feel like going out. More questions, the same answers. No one hit me again. No one raised his voice at me. It was all very polite and low-keyed. Just a little late-night spin in the car with two friends.

Finally they took me back to Manhattan and dumped me off in front of my place. Gianni leaned out of the car window toward me.

"Tonight is our little secret, sweetheart," he said. "If you tell anyone about it or report it to the police, it wouldn't be healthy for you. You see what I'm trying to say?"

I was too tired to answer. I just nodded at him and walked away. My doorman said hello. "Late night, huh, Miss Shannon?"

"You said it."

I staggered into my apartment and collapsed on the bed. After a few minutes I dragged myself into the bathroom to look in the mirror. I was a mess. My lip was already swollen and there was dried blood on my mouth. I was going to have a hard time chewing for a couple of days. On top of that, my brand new sixty dollar Gloria Vanderbilt blouse, worn special for the date with Higgins, was completely destroyed. That really depressed me.

I looked at the clock. It was nearly five-thirty in the morning. No wonder I felt awful. I had been up since the previous morning and I hadn't gotten much sleep the night before that, because of that threatening phone call. I had to be at work in less than four hours.

I wondered if Barlow would let me put in for overtime.

Chapter 8

At two the next afternoon, we were all sitting around in Dan Hodges' office—me, Dan, Barlow and Annie Klein—talking about what had happened.

What I really wanted to do was find some place to lie down and take a nap. I had spent most of the morning with the police. Ignoring Gianni's warning, I called Higgins when I got to work and told him about my little adventure. He told me to come to the stationhouse, so I trudged up there and went over my story about twelve thousand times for Higgins, Masters and the rest of the boys in the squad room. They were very interested.

"This is the first solid link that we've had that the mob is connected to the Kimberly and Luckman murders," Masters said. "It puts a whole new light on this thing."

He leaned over and looked at his notes.

"Let me go over this one more time with you," he

said. "Gianni's boys picked you up off the street about 11:30 p.m., right?"

I nodded.

"And this happened on Second Avenue, near 67th Street. Only about a block from this stationhouse. What in the hell were you doing up here at 11:30 at night, anyway?"

Higgins examined his cuticles.

"I just had dinner with a friend," I said.

"Oh, yeah? I didn't think you had any friends, Shannon. So these two take you to Gianni's hangout in Bay Ridge and he tells you Nancy Kimberly and Luckman had something that belonged to him."

"That's about it," I said. "So what happens now? Can you pin the murder on him?"

"Well, that's a problem with guys that are big in the mob. You can know something, but how you going to prove it? They bring in a battery of expensive lawyers and twenty-six witnesses who swear that the guy was taking his crippled mother to mass at the time the victim was being bumped off."

"So what good did it do to tell you all this?"

"Now don't misunderstand me. Now we have something to work with. Before we had nothing. Now we know the mob's involved. So maybe we'll get another break."

"Speaking of breaks, what about Gianni's threat to break my neck if I came to you guys?"

"You don't want police protection," Masters said. "So what are we going to do? You could press kidnapping charges; we could pick Gianni up. But he'd be out in five minutes. It would be your word against his."

"Great," I said.

"So you're too stubborn to let us protect you. So it's your funeral."

"That's just what I wanted to hear," I said bitterly.

He looked around at his men. "So what am I supposed to say?" he asked plaintively.

So now I was in Hodges' office at the *Blade* and we were still discussing the thing.

"I'm going to write it up," I said. "I'm going to write a long piece for tomorrow's paper about everything that happened last night."

"I like the idea," Dan said, "but think about it a little first. Talking to the cops is one thing. But printing it in six hundred thousand copies of a newspaper is something else. I mean, hell, Gianni may never find out you talked to the cops. They're not going to pick him up."

"Believe me, he'll find out. He probably knows already. He's very well connected."

"I still have reservations," Dan said.

"Look at it this way," I told him. "Maybe Gianni and his boys won't see the paper. I'm not sure those guys can read."

"This isn't funny, Lucy. I'm worried. It's bad enough having one of my reporters kidnapped off the goddamned street. I don't want one getting killed."

Barlow hadn't said anything but he piped up now. "I have an idea."

"Really?" I said.

"Go ahead, Walter," Hodges said. "What's your idea?"

"Why don't we run the article, but not put her name on it? We'll just say it's by an anonymous *Blade* reporter. That way we won't be drawing attention to Lucy."

"Oh, that's brilliant," I said. "Look, Walter, the only people who are going to care about this are the people who kidnapped me. And they already *know* who I am."

"Well, it was just a thought," he said.

"Anyway," I told him, "I object to the principle of it. If you want to write something, you shouldn't be afraid to put your name on it."

I looked at Hodges.

"What about the publisher?" I asked. "What does he think about all this?"

"Old man Haggerty? I haven't told him about it yet, but I'm sure he'd love you to write it. After all Lucy, you've become a celebrity in the past week. Your name's mentioned on TV news shows, in other papers—you've become a big part of the story itself. And it's selling us a lot of papers. Haggerty will go for anything that makes you more of a celebrity and sells more papers. He's not going to be worried about a little thing like the possibility of you getting your head blown off."

"What about the police protection angle?" Annie suggested. "Maybe you should change your mind about that."

"No."

"Are you sure?"

"I'm sure. Look, I don't think anything bad will

happen. By going public with this, I think we put them on the spot and they'll be afraid to try anything. They're not going to want all the publicity and headaches they'll get for knocking off a newspaper reporter. Especially one who's already told her story and named names to six hundred thousand readers. I have a gut feeling that writing about this is the thing to do, Dan," I told Hodges. "You've known me for a long time. When I get one of these gut feelings, have I ever steered you wrong?"

"Yes."

We ran the article. It went eight columns across the top of page one, with my picture and a headline: "Blade Reporter Gets Taken for a Ride by the Mob." It was a huge piece. I included everything in it, all the details, except for the part about my go-around with Les. I don't know why I didn't use that. Maybe I figured it was personal business between Les and me. Maybe I was afraid humiliating him in public might push him over the edge and force him to do something to me to save face. Anyway, I left that part out.

It was close to six p.m. by the time I finished it. I had the day off. God, did I need it. I was really dead. I stopped off on my way home at the butcher's and bought a filet mignon, and then went to an open air market on Union Square and got some salad fixings.

While I was working I drank some Scotch. By the time everything was ready, I felt pretty good. I ate ravenously while I watched the network news. The President was holding an economic summit, some

African nation had been toppled by a coup and Barbara Walters was interviewing Margaret Thatcher. Pretty boring stuff. After the news was over, *The Odd Couple* came on. That was a lot more interesting. Felix and Oscar were having a fight about redecorating their living room.

By half past eight, I had had it. I threw the dishes into the sink, undressed and crawled into bed. I was asleep in about thirty seconds. Twelve hours later I woke up feeling fit, refreshed, well-fed and generally on top of the world. No one had called me up in the middle of the night to threaten me. No one had kidnapped me and driven me to Brooklyn. No one was paying any attention to me. I wondered if I should feel hurt about it.

The phone rang. "City desk," I said.

It was Annie Klein. "You always answer your phone like that?"

"I figured it would be you guys. Who else would be calling me at this hour of the morning? And on my day off. What's up?"

"Tom Donnelly called the office trying to reach you. He wants you to be on his show this afternoon. You interested?"

"No way," I said.

Tom Donnelly had a daytime TV talk show in New York that was the No. 1 rated show of its kind. He was outspoken, controversial—it was a pretty good show. I watched it myself sometimes. He was also very big on the New York social scene. He had a lavish apartment on Central Park West and a house in Southampton, where he threw big parties in the summertime. People like Lee Radziwill,

Bianca Jagger and John Kennedy Jr. showed up there.

"He really wants you to be on," Annie said. "And Barlow thinks you should do it. He says it's good publicity for the paper."

"Look, I've had a tough week. I've been threatened, abducted, beaten up, and I've seen two dead bodies close up. I'm exhausted. I'm looking forward to spending a quiet day off. Tell Donnelly there's absolutely no way I'm going to be on his TV show."

"He says to tell you it pays five hundred dollars for a fifteen minute appearance."

"You just talked me into it."

I got to the TV studio a little after noon. Donnelly was everything I expected him to be—ruddy good looks, oozing with charm, dressed in an expensive tailor-made suit. He was very nice to me.

"You ever been on TV before?" he asked.

"A few times. Not a lot."

"Well, just be yourself and be natural and everything will be fine. A lot of people come on TV trying to be something they're not. So be yourself."

I promised I'd be myself.

Everything went pretty well. The other guests were Bella Abzug, Jerry Lewis, Elizabeth Taylor and an author who had written a book about dying. Abzug talked about the Equal Rights Amendment, Lewis talked about the Muscular Dystrophy fund, Liz talked about booze and drug problems and depression, and the author talked for fifteen minutes about death.

By the time my turn came, I decided the

audience could use some light relief. So after Donnelly introduced me as the woman reporter who defied death by taking on the Mafia in today's *Blade*, I tried the let's-look-at-the-funny-side approach.

It wasn't great, but the audience seemed to like it.

After the show Donnelly told me I was terrific. He said my personality really came across.

I said modestly that I thought Bella was the best on the show.

He said he was crazy about Bella. He said she had been at a party he gave a few weeks before and she had made mincemeat out of some male chauvinist. "It was really something," he said. "You should have been there."

"I guess my invitation got lost in the mail," I said.

As soon as I said it, I realized how it sounded. I wished I could have taken it back.

"Well, you're invited to the next one if you want to come," he said, after a slight pause.

"Look, forget about it. I was just kidding. It came out wrong."

"Well, I'm not kidding. Listen, we're having a barbecue a week from tomorrow at my place in Southampton. Nothing fancy. I really want you to come."

"I feel like a real idiot. . ."

I said I'd come.

"Good," he said. "In the meantime, how do you feel about dinner with me tonight? I'm meeting a few people at Elaine's about nine o'clock. Why don't you join us?"

"Dinner," I said. Sometimes I'm so glib it's frightening.

He said he had a couple of appointments in the early evening, but he would try to be there at nine. I should tell Elaine I was with him.

All the way home I worried about what I should wear. Elaine's is the kind of place where if Elaine doesn't like the color of your pants you can end up at a table next to the restrooms, or, worse yet, at no table at all. Of course the stars could show up wearing anything. But I was no star. Of course I was going to have dinner with one.

I decided after I got home that the key was to be casual. If you got all dressed up, everyone would think you were in town for the Elks convention. On the other hand I didn't want to look as though I just came in from baling some hay.

I took a long time getting ready and giving myself the full treatment: a restful soak in hot water with plenty of bubbles, a shampoo with conditioner, a goodly amount of Je Reviens cologne, a blow dry job on my short blonde locks and a careful brushing to keep them in place. I slipped into a red silk blouse and a full red and grey patterned skirt and white Italian sandals. I added my new grey linen one-button jacket. I fastened long rhinestone earrings into my ears and as a final touch threw on a wide-brimmed white hat. I surveyed myself in the mirror. I looked dazzling and sophisticated. All this, and brains too. It was almost heartbreaking.

I decided to take a cab. I didn't want to drive up to Elaine's in a 1971 Volkswagen.

Just as I was leaving, the phone rang. It was Ed Higgins.

"Hi," he said. "I'm glad to hear you're still alive. How'd you like to have dinner with me tonight and go to a ballgame? I've got tickets for the Yankees."

"Oh," I said, "Well..."

"I know you hate baseball, but I just put a hundred dollar bet on the Yanks and I want to check out my investment first hand. Plus you get a free dinner out of it, *and* all the hot dogs and popcorn you can eat at the game."

"I thought betting was illegal," I said.

"Yeah, I heard that. They tell me smoking pot is, too."

"Don't tell me you do that too," I said. "My God, I'll never feel the same way about the police again."

"So what do you think about tonight?"

"Gee, Ed," I said, "I wish you'd asked me earlier. I've got these other plans, and I really can't break them now."

"Okay. Listen, no problem. I know it's short notice."

"I really would like to go. I'm really sorry."

"I believe you. I'll call you again soon."

"You promise?"

"I promise."

I hung up hoping I hadn't blown it.

Donnelly was already at Elaine's when I got there. He was standing at a table chatting with

Andy Stein, the Manhattan borough president, Bobby Zarem, the public relations whiz, and Tommy Smothers, the comedian. He introduced me all around and after a little while we went over to a table reserved for us.

He asked me whether I had been to Elaine's before.

"No," I said. "The crowd I hang out with generally goes to Blimpie's."

He laughed. "Well, this is a terrific place. I think you'll like it."

"I've heard it's a bit snooty."

He unfolded his napkin carefully. "Well, it's true that Elaine is famous for snubbing people she doesn't like. But, you know, it's all part of the image. But there is a real pecking order. Anyone can have a drink at the bar. But if you want a table, you could wind up back there next to the kitchen—as far from the action and the celebrities as if you were in Iowa. It's better in the middle of the room. And the front tables are kept for people Elaine knows."

"And these?" I asked. We were sitting at one of eight tables along the wall near the entrance to the room.

"Oh, these." He smiled. "These are the best. These are for the stars."

He wasn't kidding. Tables near us were occupied by Woody Allen, Candice Bergen, Ben Gazzara and Jack Lemmon. I just spotted them in one quick glance.

"Would it be tacky if I got out my autograph

book and made the rounds?" I said.

He stared at me. "You're kidding," he said. "Right?"

"I'm kidding," I said. "Relax."

Pretty soon other people joined us. There was a big shot lawyer, a young actress, a Hollywood agent and a Broadway producer. And a lot of Big Names kept dropping by the table to chat for a while with Donnelly. Elaine herself sat down with us.

Donnelly introduced me to everyone as "Lucy Shannon, the woman you've all heard about who's been writing that devastating stuff in the *Blade* about those murders."

"You know, Tom," I said to him at one point, "that's not the only thing I've ever done. I've been a reporter for ten years, and I've written a lot of other good stuff too."

"Nonsense," he told me. "This is the only thing that matters now. No one ever heard of you before. Now you're becoming a household name. You need to take advantage of it."

"What do you mean?"

"What Tom means," the agent said, "is that this is your big break. There's definitely a hot book you can get out of all this. Possibly a movie deal too. On the book, I think the best way is to set it up with a paperback company for a quickie job so it'll get on the stands while everyone remembers your name. I can handle it for you if you want."

"I don't know," I said.

"What do you mean, you don't know? There's

One for the Money

big money for you in this. You'll be able to quit that crummy newspaper job. There's absolutely no money to be made in newspapers. Don't you all agree with that?"

Everyone at the table nodded.

"Yeah, well I sort of like it sometimes," I said. "It can be exciting, you know."

The agent reached over and patted my hand. "Forget newspapers, dear. Think books and screenplays. Okay?"

"The thing is," I said, "I don't really understand a lot about these markets. Take books, for instance. I hate most of the best sellers, and all the books I like generally sell about six copies."

"Don't worry about that," he said. "I can tell you what to write. I know all about the market. That's my job."

"You don't understand," I said. "I've thought at times about writing a book. But when I do, I want to write one that's important to me, that I care about. I don't just want to try to write something that you think will make some money. That's not what really matters to me. Do you understand what I mean?"

Everyone was staring at me as if I'd just dropped in from Jupiter.

"Does anyone want another drink?" Donnelly asked quickly.

I told him I did. Badly.

We hung out there engaging in that sort of intellectual chit chat until about 2:30 a.m. Then we all said goodbye. Everyone said they were glad to meet me.

"You got a car?" Donnelly asked me when we were out on Second Avenue.

"No. I took a cab."

"Well, let me give you a lift downtown."

"So what did you think of it all?" he asked me, as we drove off in his dark blue Mercedes.

"You want an honest reaction," I said.

"Of course I do."

"I thought your friends were full of shit."

"Hey!" He gave a sudden laugh. "That's too honest."

We rode in silence for a while.

"Listen," he said, "do you have to get home right away or can you come up for a nightcap? To my place."

I thought about it for a minute.

"Sure," I said. "I can come up to your place."

We went up to his place.

His place wasn't all that impressive, I guess—if you're used to hanging out at Buckingham Palace or the Rockefeller estate in Pocantico Hills. It was only a little bigger than Grand Central Station and the furniture couldn't have cost more than a hundred thousand dollars. There were abstract paintings, primitive carvings and a huge window wall that overlooked Central Park.

"Hey, this place is okay," I said. "Reminds me of home."

By now we were both hungry, so he ordered some sandwiches from an all-night deli and we ate them and drank Cokes while we watched a W.C. Fields movie on the late show. Then we discussed Fields for a while.

The inevitable seduction scene followed. He kissed me once. Then he kissed me again. Then he came at me in a way that reminded me of an experience I once had in the back seat of a 1957 DeSoto. When the going got hot and heavy he paused, brushed the hair out of my eyes and whispered, "Do you want to go into the bedroom?"

I said yes.

The huge bed faced another window wall overlooking Central Park. After we made love, he vanished for a few minutes and then came back carrying a bottle of champagne and two glasses. We sat up against the fat pillows, drinking and chatting about this and that. Then we made love again. After that, understandably tuckered out, he rolled over and went to sleep.

I tried to sleep, but I couldn't. Finally I sat up in bed, pulled my knees up to my chest and smoked a cigarette. The bed had a sort of ebony wall behind it, with built-in bookcases and cupboards and reading lights and low ebony tables on either side of it. Outside the sky was paling to dawn. I looked at Donnelly, sleeping peacefully next to me.

Jesus Christ, I thought, what am I doing here?

Chapter 9

I woke up at nine the next morning. Donnelly was still asleep. It was Saturday and he had told me he rarely got up before noon on weekends. I took a shower in the palatial bathroom and pulled last night's clothes back on. I left a note on my pillow saying I had had to go to work.

I had a quick breakfast in a nearby coffee shop and phoned the city desk. Barlow answered. He wanted to know whether I was coming in. He said it was quiet so I told him I wanted to check out some things on the Kimberly story. He said that Karen Tunney, the girl in the record shop, had been trying to get in touch with me. She had left her number.

She answered on the first ring. Nothing was up, she just wanted to tell me how much she liked my article in the *Blade*. She thought I had guts.

"I think you've got guts yourself," I said. "I don't know whether you've noticed it, but you're the only person left alive who worked at Stereo Heaven."

"Unless Janet turns up," she said.

"Listen, could we get together for a talk? Are you still working at the store?"

No, she said, the store was closed. John Luckman had owned it and lawyers were working on the whole thing. So she was out of work and planning to apply for unemployment. She could get along for a year or so on that, and on drawing up astrological charts for people. "Is there anything special you want to talk about?" she asked.

I told her I thought if we went over it again we might stumble on something. She didn't think so, but she was happy to talk to me. She lived in the Village.

"Today's a bad day for me," she said. "I've got a million things I have to do. How about tomorrow? Maybe we could have dinner around here. About six o'clock."

That was fine with me. She gave me her address: Jane Street just off Eighth Avenue. The ninth floor.

I hung up and took a cab over to Janet Langmann's place on 80th Street. Just for something to do, I rang her bell in the lobby. No answer. I wasn't going to get an easy exclusive today. After awhile, I buzzed the super's number.

A fat, balding man wearing a green work suit and smoking a cigar poked his head out of a first floor apartment. All New York supers seem to be fat, balding men who wear green work suits and smoke cigars. Sometimes I think before they become supers they have to go to a training school somewhere—like airline stewardesses—and learn to look alike.

"My name is Lucy Shannon," I told him. "I'm a reporter for the *Blade*."

"So?" he said. He didn't seem impressed. I wasn't used to that.

"Has anyone besides the police been around here in the last few days asking about Janet Langmann in 4A?"

"Yeah. About a hundred nosy reporters, just like you."

"Besides reporters," I asked, "anyone else?"

"Listen, I'm going to tell you the same thing I told them others. Nothing. I don't know nothing. I don't want to know nothing. So leave me alone. If I catch you hanging around here again, I'm going to call the cops."

He slammed the door in my face.

I went outside. It had rained during the night, but the sun was shining brightly. A great day for the beach. Or for a picnic. Or for strolling hand-in-hand with someone through Central Park. I bought all the Saturday papers from a newsstand on First Avenue, and walked back across the street from the apartment house. I made myself comfortable on a low wall and read the papers, glancing up occasionally to see who was going in or coming out of the building. I didn't know exactly why I was sitting there. I was waiting for something to happen. Anything.

I did the crossword puzzle in the *Times* and then I did the one in the *Blade*, and the Scrabble game in the *Post* and the Jumble words in the *Daily News*. I read the news sections, the entertainment sections and the editorial pages, including letters to the editor. I was almost at the point of reading the society pages to find out who was vacationing this month in Palm Springs but I decided I wasn't that desperate yet. Once a Con Ed crew stopped to do some manhole work directly in front of the building. I was pretty sure that was not important, but I wrote it down in my notebook anyway. It was something to do.

After hours of this, I came to one inescapable conclusion. I was hungry. I strolled down the street to a pizza stand and got a double cheese with pepperoni and a large Pepsi. While I was walking back with this to my wall, a truck went through a puddle left over from last night's rain and splashed mud on my skirt. Then while I was eating the pizza a big hunk of cheese dropped onto my blouse and left a big stain.

Altogether my sophisticated image was noticeably battered. I hoped none of my friends from Elaine's would pass by. I'd probably lose my place in the Social Register.

Meaningless people passed in and out of Janet's building. A group of construction workers rode by in a truck and made obscene sucking noises at me. Three other men tried to pick me up—one guy obviously mistook me for a hooker. I just kept my eye on the building.

By six o'clock the Saturday strollers and shoppers were heading home to enjoy Saturday night. Dinner, a movie, a few drinks, maybe a little dancing. How did you spend Saturday night, Shannon? Oh, I watched a building.

I wasn't sure how much longer I should stick it out. If I didn't get home soon, I was going to miss *Love Boat*.

Finally, a little after 7:30, something happened. A brown Lincoln pulled up and parked in front of the building. I moved quickly out of sight behind a pillar, leaving the debris of my vigil behind: newspapers, paper cups, pizza box. Somebody stayed at the wheel and the other guy in the front seat got out and went inside. I slid from behind the pillar and ran down to a pay phone in the pizza parlor. I called the cops.

"I want to talk to Lt Masters or Sgt Higgins," I said.

"Neither one is here now. Can I help you?"

"Okay, my name is Lucy Shannon. I'm a reporter from the *Blade* and I've been working with the police on the Nancy Kimberly case."

"Uh huh."

"I'm at Janet Langmann's apartment house, 441 East 80th Street, between First and York. She's the missing girl. I think someone's gone up to her apartment. You got that address?

"May I ask what you are doing there, ma'am?"

"I've been staking it out. All afternoon."

"Staking it out?"

"Yeah, you know, watching it. Look, it's too complicated to go into right now. You got that address?"

"First and 48th. . ."

"No, no. First and 80th. 441 East 80th Street. Apartment 4A. Please get someone over here right away. I don't know how long these guys will hang around. One is waiting in the car."

I hung up and ran back. The brown Lincoln was still there. I wrote down the license number.

Five minutes passed. Ten minutes. Fifteen minutes. I kept looking down the street for the flashing lights of a police car. Nothing. Finally the guy came back out. He got inside and slammed the door and after a minute the car eased off down 80th, took a right on York, and disappeared.

I walked slowly across the street. In the lobby, I pushed the super's buzzer. He came out smoking another cigar and still wearing his green outfit.

"You again?" he said. "I warned you. If you don't get out of here, I'll call the cops."

"I've already called them," I said. "And now I think you'd better open up Apartment 4A."

At that moment, three cars full of New York's Finest pulled up to the front door. Masters came in first.

I looked at him in disgust. "You guys didn't break any speed records getting here, did you? They're gone now."

"There was a mixup," he said.

"A mixup?"

"Yeah. The guy who took your call thought you were a nut. They contacted me on the West Side, and I got here as fast as I could. What happened?"

I told him about the two men in the brown Lincoln that had followed me home one night.

"You never told me about any brown Lincoln following you home," he said.

"I'm telling you now."

One for the Money

Masters turned to the super. "Okay buddy, let's open 4A and find out if it's had any visitors recently."

The super grunted something unintelligible and got his keys.

When we got there, we didn't need them. Someone had jimmied the lock and the door was open. Inside it looked like a cyclone had hit the place. Furniture was tipped over, drawers emptied on the floor, the futon slit open.

"Jeez, look at this place," Masters said. "What a mess. Somebody was really looking for something."

While the police went through the rubble searching for clues and dusting for fingerprints, I called the office. I told them what happened and said I'd be in in about twenty minutes to write a story for the Sunday morning editions. Masters promised to call me if they turned up anything there. He didn't expect to. It looked like a very professional job.

I took a cab down to the *Blade*. On my way, I stopped at a McDonald's and got a couple of cheeseburgers, some french fries and a chocolate milk shake. I ate at my desk while I worked. Pizza for lunch, McDonald's for dinner. I ought to will my stomach to science when I die.

When I was about halfway through the story, Masters called.

"I'm back at the stationhouse," he said. "We didn't really find anything worth mentioning at the scene."

"I didn't think you would."

"There is one thing, though. That license plate you gave us on the Lincoln. We just got back the results of a check on it. Who do you think the car's registered to?"

"Tony Gianni," I said.

"Right. Or to one of his people, anyway."

"What are you going to do?"

"I just sent some of my men over to pick up Gianni and his boys."

"Do you think you can hit him with any kind of charge that'll stick?"

"I don't know," Masters said. "But we certainly can hold them overnight for questioning. I think it's time to try and find out just what Mr. Gianni knows about this case."

Chapter 10

The phone rang and woke me out of a sound sleep. I reached over and knocked the whole thing onto the floor. It took me a few seconds to find it.

"Yeah?" I said finally.

"You okay?"

It was Higgins.

"More or less. Mornings aren't my best time of day."

"Jesus, it sounded like I was going to have to send an Emergency Rescue unit over there for you."

"What time is it?" I asked.

"About ten o'clock."

I groaned.

"Sorry. I guess I shouldn't have called so early. Anyway, I wondered if you'd like to come uptown later and have breakfast with me. I'll be finishing up at work soon."

"What day is today?"

"Sunday."

"And what was your offer again?"

"Breakfast. I'm at the stationhouse now. I thought you could come up here, we'd talk a bit about the case and then go out and get something to eat."

"Wait a minute," I said. "Is this call personal or professional?"

"Well, actually it's both. But the personal part is a lot bigger than the professional part."

I laughed. "I'll accept that," I said.

"I heard you had some more excitement last night."

"A bit. Did Masters pick up Gianni?"

"Right."

"So what happened?"

"That is one of the things I wanted to talk to you about."

"You don't want to tell me on the phone?"

"We'll talk later. How about eleven o'clock or so?"

"Okay," I said. "See you then."

After I hung up, I went into the bathroom to take a shower. I was just getting ready to turn on the water when the phone rang again. I wrapped a towel around me and walked back into the bedroom to answer it.

"Hi, Lucy. This is Tom Donnelly."

"Hi, Tom Donnelly."

"I read your story in the paper this morning. All day stakeout. Mobsters invading the home of the missing Langmann girl. You were a busy young lady after you left me yesterday morning, weren't you?"

"Yeah. You got my note, didn't you?"

"Sure. I can't say I wasn't disappointed that you weren't there when I woke up."

"You know us career girls. Always on the move."

"Well anyway, I'm out at my place here on the Island, and I was reading your article over breakfast. I had to call to tell you I was impressed. That was a really nice piece of detective work."

"I was lucky," I said.

"You're not suddenly getting modest on me, are you?"

"I'm just being honest. It was really just luck that I was there when those mobsters showed up. I could sit out in front of that building a hundred times, and probably nothing would happen. This one time it did."

"Maybe so, but I'm still impressed. How are you doing otherwise?"

"Okay, I guess. It's been a rough week or so."

"That's one of the reasons I called. How'd you like to come out to my place? We could do some swimming, take a walk, cook a good meal outside. You could relax, forget about murders and mobsters and stuff like that."

"Today?"

"Sure. I can have someone pick you up in the city. You could be here in a couple hours. We could drive back together tonight."

"It sounds great, but I'm afraid I have other plans."

"Break them."

I thought for a minute.

"I can't. They're not really personal plans. Even though it's my day off, I sort of have to do some work today on the Kimberly case."

Why did I say that? Why didn't I just tell him I was having breakfast with someone I'm dating?

"Oh. I'm sorry."

"Me too."

"Well, I'll call you in a day or so."

"Sure. Sounds good."

"And you're still on for the barbecue out here next Saturday, aren't you? Don't forget about that."

"Forget about it. Are you kidding? I've been going over my old Girl Scout manual trying to remember how to start a campfire. By the way, should I bring my own marshmallows?"

He laughed. "It's not exactly that kind of barbecue."

"Somehow I knew it wasn't."

I managed to make it into the shower without the phone ringing again. If things didn't let up, I was going to have to hire an appointments secretary. I'd only been awake thirty minutes, and I'd already had two offers for dates. Neither Warren Beatty nor Burt Reynolds had called me yet, but it was still early.

I spent a long time in the shower. It had been a tough night. I'd stayed at the *Blade* working on my story until nearly midnight. Then some *Blade* people asked me to have a drink with them. I remember going to a bar around the corner for a while. Then I remember someone saying we should

One for the Money

go uptown to some other bar near the *Daily News* and see who was there. I don't remember a whole lot after that. But I woke up with a terrific hangover.

After I got out of the shower, I felt better. Not good. But better. I drank about six cups of coffee, pulled on some clothes and eventually headed out to meet Higgins. I rode the subway uptown, figuring I could put it down on my expense account as cab fare and come out a few bucks ahead. I was saving up to buy a yacht.

At the 67th Street stationhouse, the cop at the door asked me who I wanted to see.

"The Homicide Squad," I said. "Sgt Higgins."

He pointed a big, beefy finger at the stairwell. "Up there," he said. "Second floor."

"You don't have to tell me. I've spent so much time in this place the past week I'm thinking of having my mail forwarded here."

Higgins was sitting at his desk with his feet up on an open drawer, staring absent-mindedly out of the grimy second floor window.

"You working today?" I asked. "Is that what I pay you my tax dollars to do all day?"

"Hi," he said. "Glad you could come. Sit down."

He motioned to a chair next to his desk.

"The thing is," he said, "Gianni came in here last night and told us some stuff—most of it undoubtedly lies. I'd like to go over it with you. I know you've done this before, but just bear with us one more time."

"Can I ask you one question first?"

"Sure."

"Is this the professional part?"

"What?"

"You said when you asked me to come up here that it was partly personal and partly professional. This is the professional part, huh? You'll tell me when we get to the personal part, won't you? I don't want to miss it."

"You'll be the first to know."

Masters stuck his head into the room.

"Have you talked to her yet?" he asked Higgins.

"I was just getting to it, Lieutenant."

"Okay," Masters said to me, "I want you to tell Sgt Higgins everything you know about this case. Everything. Do you understand me? And just answer his questions straight, Shannon. Never mind your smart ass remarks. Christ, am I tired of them."

He disappeared.

"What's the matter with him?" I asked Higgins. "Maybe you should let him work somebody over with a rubber hose for a while. It'd probably make him feel better."

"The Lieutenant had a rough night," Higgins said.

"Gianni? You mean he couldn't pin enough on him to arrest him for murder."

"He couldn't pin enough on him to arrest him for jaywalking. We had him here for six hours, and all he did was keep asking us who Nancy Kimberly was. He says he never heard of her."

"Doesn't he read the newspapers?"

"We asked him that. He said he was too busy"

"Yeah," I said. "I guess that sand and gravel business keeps you hopping all the time. What about kidnapping me? What does he say about that?"

"Ah, that was one of the highlights of the evening."

"What do you mean?"

"He says it never happened."

"He says he never talked to me about the case?"

"Oh no, he admits he talked to you. But he tells a little different story from you."

"What's his story?" I asked.

"You're not going to like it."

"Try me."

"Okay," he said, "This is it. According to Gianni, you kept pestering him for days about wanting to meet him somewhere to talk. You left messages all over town. Finally, he says, just to get you off his back he agreed to see you, and you said you'd wait for him on the corner of 67th and Second Avenue. Gianni sent a car to pick you up there and take you out to Brooklyn. So you came out there and asked him a lot of crazy questions about Nancy Kimberly. He didn't have any idea what you were talking about and he kept telling you that. You started ranting and raving and accusing him of all sorts of things. He said you were hysterical. He says he thinks you're emotionally unstable."

"He said that?" I said. "I feel awful. Here I thought I made such a good impression on him."

"So they finally got you calmed down and drove

you home to Manhattan. He didn't even think any more about it until he read what you wrote in the paper the next day. He was stunned. He can't understand why you would make up all those things. He figures either you're running out of material or you've been working too hard."

"Is that it? That's all of it?"

"No, there's something else. He says you went berserk in his office and attacked one of his associates. Just walked over and kicked the guy in the groin for no reason at all. He's thinking of filing suit for assault. It seems this poor guy has been suffering since then from acute pain and emotional trauma. He can't work and he can't sleep and his family life has gone down the tubes." He looked at me. "Did you really do that, Lucy?"

"There was a small altercation," I said. I told him about it.

"You should have told us this before. The Lieutenant wasn't too happy to find out about it from Gianni. You can understand his point of view."

"What happens now?" I asked. "I mean is that all that's going to happen here? Gianni waltzes in, gives you this bullshit story and then waltzes out again? You haven't got anything on him?"

"What do you think?" he said.

"I've been thinking about it," I said. "There's something Karen Tunney told me last week. I was asking her about John Luckman and she said he had kind of a nasty temper. Some woman left a briefcase in the store by accident and I guess

Luckman or Nancy picked it up, and when Karen asked him about it he blew up at her. She says that was the last day Nancy worked at the store. I didn't think much about it at the time..."

"But now you think there might have been something in that briefcase that was valuable. Something that could have gotten a couple of people killed." He made some notes. "It's certainly worth looking into. I'll send somebody over to talk to Karen."

"I'm having dinner with her tonight. I'll ask her about it and I'll get right back to you."

"Okay," he said. "How do you feel about breakfast?"

Masters was standing next to a coffee machine in the hallway. He took a big gulp from his cup and made a face. Then he saw us. "Where the hell do you two think you're going?" he said.

"Intensive personal interrogation," Higgins said. "That's what we need to break this case."

Masters took another gulp and crumpled his cup into a little ball. He flipped it into a waste can and walked away, shaking his head.

"Unbelievable," he muttered. "Un-fucking-believable."

When we reached the street Higgins put his arms around me and kissed me.

"Wait a minute," I said. "Don't tell me. This is the personal part, right?"

Hs kissed me again.

"This is the personal part," he said.

We stayed on the sidewalk there doing a lot of

kissing. I came up for air after a few minutes and put my hands on the sides of his face and looked at him.

"I have a thought," I said. "After I have dinner with Karen Tunney tonight, why don't you drop over to my place? You're not working tonight, are you?"

"No," he said. "I can be there. Was there anything special you had in mind to do?"

"I'm sure we'll think of something," I said.

We had a long breakfast at a place on Third Avenue; we lingered drinking coffee and talking. Higgins said he would come to my place about ten that night.

I had some time before I had to meet Karen Tunney. I took a subway downtown to the Village and browsed in some bookstores and boutiques. Then I read the Sunday *Times* on a bench in Washington Park. Street musicians were playing, kids were tossing frisbees, couples were making out on the grass and drug dealers were making sales. Just a lazy summer afternoon in New York City.

While I was strolling through the Village streets I thought I saw a car following me. The driver was double-parked a little behind me. He could have been waiting for a parking space. Or he could have been one of Gianni's boys keeping an eye on me. Or maybe the cops were tailing me after all? Or the guy could have been looking for a parking space. I was getting a little paranoid.

I got to Jane Street a few minutes after six. Karen Tunney's apartment house was a sort of dilapidated ten story building. There was a little crowd gathered on the corner.

There's this thing about crowds or accidents or fires that attracts reporters. We simply can't just walk by them. If I'm sitting in a restaurant and a police car pulls up outside, I go out and take a look. I've driven a lot of dates crazy that way. Someone once told me that if a fire truck went by during my wedding, I'd probably run out of the church and chase it. I walked over to see what was going on.

A young cop was standing in the middle of the crowd.

"What happened?" I said to him.

"A jumper," he said.

"Dead?"

"Yeah. We're just waiting for an ambulance to come and take the body away."

"Who was it?" I asked.

"We don't know. Some woman."

He pointed to something lying on the street, covered with a blanket. The cop's partner was standing next to it. In the distance, I could hear the wail of a siren. The ambulance was on its way. It might as well take its time. It didn't matter now.

I took out my press card and showed it to the cop.

"My name is Lucy Shannon. I'm a reporter with the *Blade*. Do you mind if I take a look at the body?"

He shrugged.

"Why not?" he said. "She's not going to mind."

We walked over and he lifted the blanket.

They say that if a person falls from really high

up—thirty floors or so—the body's almost unrecognizable. Just a mass of blood, skin and bones. Hardly human. This one wasn't that bad, although it certainly wasn't pretty. You could still tell that it was a woman. You could still tell that she had been young and even kind of pretty. You could still tell that this was Karen Tunney.

I went across the street as fast as I could. I like to think I'm tough, but I didn't feel so tough then. Mostly I felt like I was going to be sick. I held onto a light pole to steady myself, and took some deep breaths. It took a few minutes for me to get myself together enough to walk back to the building.

The door to her apartment was open. Just like John Luckman's. Don't go in there, Shannon, I told myself. Tony Gianni or Les or Rocky might be waiting in there. You could get your head blown off. It's a police job. I thought about this while I was walking into the apartment.

Everything seemed perfectly normal: living room, kitchen, bedroom, bathroom. A window in the living room was wide open. I would have bet my year's salary that she didn't do it herself. Somebody threw her out of that window. I was sure of it.

I'd only met her that one time, and talked to her on the phone briefly yesterday morning. I didn't really know her. She said she thought I was gutsy, and I said the same about her. She offered to do my horoscope. She was looking forward to taking some time off and living for a while on unemployment. And now she was dead. Goodbye, Karen Tunney.

And what about me? If I had gotten there ten

minutes earlier I might be lying on the pavement next to her. There might be somebody waiting for me outside now. It wasn't a comforting thought.

I picked up the phone and called Masters. After I told him about it, I called the *Blade* city desk. Jim McKenna answered. He was a rewriteman who sometimes filled in on Sunday as night city editor. Sundays are slow, so the paper operates with a skeleton staff to cover parades, street festivals—that sort of thing.

"What've you got?" he asked. "Cat stuck in a tree in Brooklyn? Somebody win a three-legged race at a picnic? Nothing but biggies on Sunday night."

I told him what I had and he let out a long low whistle of surprise. He said he would call Barlow and Hodges and send some people over right away. Then he put me on to a rewriteman.

Chapter 11

Before leaving, I decided to check the apartment once more. Nothing exciting in the kitchen—just a lot of wheat germ, granola, fruit juice and yogurt. In the living room were a few sticks of furniture that had seen better days, a bookshelf filled with astrology and physical fitness titles and, resting against the wall, a ten-speed bicycle. That was it. No clues. No appointment book with a name penciled in just before mine. No name scrawled on the wall in blood. No monogrammed cufflinks torn off in a struggle. How come I couldn't seem to get a break? It was never this tough for Hercule Poirot.

An army of police was already on the street when I came back downstairs. I didn't see Masters. A couple of plainclothes detectives were talking to people in the crowd, trying to find witnesses.

"Is Lt Masters here?" I asked them.

They turned to look at me. One was a big, beefy guy, the other was tall and skinny with short cropped hair right out of the 1950s. Both looked like no-nonsense cops, real tough guys. They eyed me suspiciously.

"Who's asking?" the beefy one said belligerently.

I was in no mood for a fight. I decided to be polite.

"I'm the one who called him. I've just been up in the dead girl's apartment," I said.

The big one moved quickly over to me.

"Oh yeah?" he said. "So tell us—what were you doing in her apartment?"

"Look, it's okay. My name is Lucy Shannon. I'm a reporter for the *Blade*."

"You got any proof of that?" the thin one asked.

I took my press card out of my handbag. He stared at it for a long time. I was getting tired of being polite.

"Is that enough proof that I'm a reporter? I'd show you my typewriter ribbon too, but I left it back at the office."

He handed me back my press card without smiling.

"So you're a reporter," he said. "I recognize the name, I know you've been writing about the case. But that still doesn't explain what you were doing in the dead girl's apartment. You got an explanation for that?"

"I can see I can't hide anything from you," I said. "The truth is that I was selling *Blade* subscriptions door-to-door in the building. I tried to sell the dead woman on a twenty-six week special, but she only wanted the thirteen-week deal. We argued, one thing led to another and finally I threw her out of the ninth floor window. Then I came down here and told you guys how I'd just been up in the apartment as a clever ploy to throw suspicion off myself. Then I was going to melt away in the crowd."

"You're a regular riot, lady," the thin cop said. "I think I'm going to die laughing."

"C'mon," I said. "This is getting us nowhere. Is Masters around here anywhere? He'll straighten this out."

"You looking for me?" a voice said.

I turned around. Masters was puffing on a big cigar and staring at the body under the blanket. He looked like a guy in a poker game who keeps losing every hand and can't figure out why it's happening or what to do about it. I knew the feeling. I felt the same way myself.

The cops sprang to attention.

"Evening, Lieutenant."

Masters grunted at them. "You," he said, pointing at me. "Over here."

We walked a few feet away.

"Your boys were giving me a hard time," I said.

"Hard to believe," Masters said. "I can't imagine why anyone would want to give a hard time to a sweetie like you. But maybe it's not you; maybe they don't care for your paper."

"Possible," I said. "They're unhappy with our policy on Lebanon, maybe."

I told him everything that had happened, starting with the telephone conversation with Karen yesterday morning.

"She didn't say anything at all about what she might be doing before she met you? And you don't think she was the kind of girl who might decide to go out a window like that? So who do you think would help her jump?"

"Gianni," I said. "One of his goons."

"We'll talk to Gianni again," Masters said. "And he'll have a helluva straight alibi. He always does. You can bet he was having dinner with a parish priest or visiting sick kids in an orphanage this afternoon."

"So, you have any brilliant ideas about why she was killed?" I asked.

"Offhand, I'd say it had something to do with the fact she worked at Stereo Heaven. Of course, that's just a wild guess."

"I can see why they call you a trained investigator, Lieutenant."

"Well, there's one good thing about all this. Assuming Stereo Heaven is the link—which it seems like it has to be—then this has to be the end of the murders," he said.

"Why?"

"Because everyone who worked at Stereo Heaven is dead. There's no one left to kill."

"What about Janet Langmann?" I asked. "Anything new on her?"

"No. Nothing."

"You're certain that she's dead too, aren't you?"

I said. "You just said there was no one left to kill from Stereo Heaven."

Masters didn't say anything.

"You're sure Janet Langmann's dead too, aren't you?" I asked again.

"Let's go upstairs," he said.

The cops were going over the apartment with a fine tooth comb. One of them called Masters over to the open window facing the street. He pointed to the floor. I looked down and saw what seemed to be a small red stain.

"Blood?" Masters asked.

The crime lab people came over and checked the spot out carefully. After a few minutes one of them stood up and showed something to Masters. He grunted.

"Find something?" I asked.

"Some hairs. You knew her," Masters said. "What color was her hair?"

"Blonde."

"Right," he said. "Blonde." He pushed his hat back on his head. "Somebody came up here before you did. Somehow they got in here, and walloped her on the head with a heavy object. She falls nine storeys to the street so she's dead then for sure. But that head laceration tells us she was dead before she went out the window."

I hung around for a while, but nothing else seemed to come up in the way of evidence so I went back down to the street. It was pretty crowded. Lots of reporters and TV crews were there, along with policemen and people who lived on the block.

I called the office from a pay phone near the corner of Eighth Avenue. Dan came on the line. He was waiting for me. Before he gave me to rewrite, he told me they had already put a special replate edition on the press with a Page One bulletin about the murder. He was going to use my new information for a second replate special.

"Get down here and write the complete story for the next regular edition at 10:40," he said. "You've got ninety minutes."

"I'm on my way," I said.

I found a group of *Blade* reporters and photographers in the crowd. One of the photographers was just rushing back to the office to process a roll of film for the next edition so I hitched a ride with him. We roared across Canal Street to the East Side, through Chinatown and got to the *Blade* building in seven minutes flat. I think we set a record.

I had never seen so many people in the city room on a Sunday. Barlow, Hodges, reporters, rewritemen, photographers, editors. They all crowded around me for the story. I was a celebrity.

Hodges came over and growled at us.

"What is this—show and tell? We've got a newspaper to get out here. Let's break this up." He looked at the clock. "You've got twenty-five minutes," he said to me. "Stop talking and start writing."

The crowd dispersed and I sat down hastily at a computer terminal.

"Don't try to make like Hemingway," he said.

"We don't need that here. Just make it quick and simple. Hand it to me a few paragraphs at a time."

I did what he said. Wrote quickly, punched in the command to save it, called a copy boy to get a printout and run it over to Dan Hodges. I went on like that until by deadline I had written about twenty-five inches of copy: everything I knew. Hodges finished editing it, sent it on to a copy editor and came over to me. I was gulping a fast cup of coffee.

"Tired?" he asked, smiling.

"Just taking a coffee break," I said. "It's in my contract."

"Well, we're not finished yet. There's two more editions to go."

"Okay, I'm game."

"What I need from you now is a first person account of how it all looked to you. Your feelings when you saw the body, your recollections about the times you talked to the dead girl, all that stuff. Say whatever you want, just let everything out—lots of feeling, lots of emotion. I want it to bring tears to my eyes."

"How long do I have to write this great piece of literature?"

"Thirty minutes."

"Thirty minutes. C'mon, Dan. I need more time than that if you want me to turn out the kind of thing you're looking for. No one could do it in thirty minutes. I know I'm good, but I'm not that good."

"You better stop talking and start writing," he said. "Now you've only got twenty-nine minutes."

Somehow I got it written in time. It was not great prose, but then very little great prose appears in a newspaper. Barlow read it quickly, made a few small editing changes and then passed it on to be put into print.

"That's fine, Lucy," he said. "Just what I wanted."

"Did it make you cry?" I said.

"Now that you're finished, I'll tell you a secret. I never cry."

"You will when you get my overtime bill. Today's supposed to be my day off."

"I may be wrong," he said, "but I have the feeling you'd pay me to work on this story."

"No comment," I said.

The layout sheets for the paper were on the desk in front of him.

"What else have you done on the Kimberly case?" I asked.

"A lot. Egan has written an entire history of the case, starting with the first murder and including every detail we have. It runs over a hundred inches long and takes up two whole pages. Tom Gilroy, the police reporter, has done a piece on the growing pressure on the Police Department to come up with a break in the case—the Commissioner's apparently furious about these new bodies that keep popping up. We've got somebody trying to go back and get an interview with Janet Langmann's mother on the lonely wait for word on her daughter. There's a whole page of pictures. And a Page One editorial urging any New Yorker who knows anything about the case to come forward and tell the police. The *Blade's* offering a five thousand dollar reward for information."

"Wow," I said. "We're pulling out all the stops, huh?"

"Yeah. If you don't care about the Kimberly case, there's not going to be much for you to read in tomorrow's *New York Blade*."

"I don't think there's anybody left in this town who doesn't care about the Nancy Kimberly case," I said.

I decided to wait for an edition of the paper with both of my stories in it. Annie Klein and I sat around the city desk, sipping coffee and munching on doughnuts that somebody had brought back to the office. I was ravenous. It suddenly dawned on me that I hadn't eaten since breakfast. After a while, a copy editor came by and dropped off copies of the final edition of the paper. Both my stories were on page one.

"Pretty impressive," Annie said. "You're a real star."

"Right now I'm just hungry and very sleepy," I said. "What time is it?"

She looked at her watch. "12:30 a.m. Why? You got some good-looking guy waiting for you back at your place?"

I slapped my forehead. "Jesus, I forgot," I said.

"Forgot what?"

"That cop on the case I told you about—Ed Higgins. He was supposed to come to my apartment at ten. In all the excitement, I never gave it a thought. He probably has no idea what happened."

"Is it too late to call him?" Annie asked.

"I hope not," I said.

Chapter 12

Higgins picked up the phone on the second ring.
"Guess who?" I said.
He didn't say anything.
"Are you mad at me?"
"Who me? Mad? Don't be silly. Why should it make anyone mad to be stood up for a date?"
"You're mad," I said. "I'm pretty perceptive."
"Nah, you got it all wrong, it was a great evening. Let me tell you how much fun I had. First, I banged on your door for a real long time. Then I dialed your number from a pay phone on the corner and let it ring for about ten minutes. Finally I went back and hung out in your lobby for an hour or so, making intellectual chitchat with your doorman while I waited. He's a terrific conversationalist, your doorman. He told me all about his hernia operation."
"You haven't listened to any news, have you?"
"No, I just got home about a half hour ago."
"Karen Tunney was murdered last night. I got to

her place just after it happened. I've been there and then at the office all night."

There was a long pause.

"My God," he said. "What happened?"

I went through the whole thing again.

"I'm worried about you," he said.

"That makes two of us. Listen, maybe we can still get together? The night, as they say, is young."

He gave me his address on Riverside Drive and 86th Street.

I hung up and looked around for Annie Klein. She was still sitting at the city desk reading the paper.

"Hey Annie," I said, "can I get a lift uptown with you?"

She looked up. "What's the matter? Your engine blow up again?"

"I didn't drive today. And for your information, there's nothing wrong with my car. It just has a few miles on it."

"It's a heap of junk. Why don't you break down and buy a new one?"

"I can't afford it," I said. "I've suffered a few financial reverses lately."

"Stocks?"

"No, Bloomingdale's. I owe them for eight hundred dollars worth of clothes and they're starting to talk about things like collection agencies and lawsuits. Plus my cash machine just ate my Mastercharge and I can't get it back until I pay that bill, too."

Annie shook her head and sighed.

One for the Money 125

"You really ought to try and get your life together, Lucy. Okay, let's go. I'm headed up the East Side. Where do you want me to let you off?"

I cleared my throat.

"Actually," I said, "I have to go over to the West Side. Riverside Drive and 86th."

Annie shrugged her shoulders. "Sorry. Like I said, I'm going up the East Side. If you want to come along and then catch a ride across town somewhere, that's fine."

She picked up the paper and her purse, getting ready to leave.

"Annie, give me a break, huh?" I said. "It'd just take you an extra fifteen minutes or so to run me across town. It's really important. I've kept this guy waiting all night."

"Look, Lucy, this may come as a surprise to you, but I'm an editor here—one of your bosses, if you want to look at it that way—not your chauffeur. If you don't want to come with me, then take a cab or a subway. I don't care, I'm leaving."

I followed her out of the city room.

"There are no cabs downtown now," I shouted. "And you can't be serious about taking the subway all the way up there. Nobody rides subways at this time of night except derelicts and muggers. If I got mugged, you'd never forgive yourself."

"I'd get over it," she said.

"Annie, listen to me, this is a really big date. Consider it a personal favor I'm asking you for. Remember all the things I've done for you."

"Like what?" She stopped and turned to face me.

"Like... like, well, how about the time you were just starting out on the desk, and a reporter screwed up a City Council story that got past you and onto Page One? Remember how Hodges blamed you for the mistake and wanted to fire you for it? Who was it that went to Hodges and told him it wasn't really your fault? And who was it that convinced him not to fire you? Me, that's who."

Annie stared at me incredulously.

"Yeah, and who was the reporter that screwed up the story in the first place?" she said. "You, that's who."

"Well, maybe that wasn't a very good example. But remember the time..."

"Enough, already, I'll take you," she said, throwing up her hands. "I'll take you wherever you want to go. Just don't walk me down memory lane anymore."

I was properly grateful. We headed down the hall toward the elevators.

"So how do you feel after everything that happened tonight?" she asked me. "Scared?"

"It's a funny thing," I said. "I nearly fainted when I saw that body on the street. I mean I was almost sick. But then it was this big story and the adrenalin started pumping. Up until now I felt detached from the whole thing—asking questions, looking around, writing... Now it's beginning to hit me that I'm involved in this thing."

I told her about the brown Lincoln and the phone call.

"Jesus," she said. "It's Gianni."

"Yeah. The same car I saw outside Janet Langmann's building. They traced it to Gianni."

"If they're watching you," she said, "how long will they watch? What do they want? You ought to give up the John Wayne act and get the cops to look after you. Maybe they trailed Karen Tunney for a while too. And in the end..."

"In the end they killed her," I said.

It was still stifling hot outside. It took a few minutes to adjust to the shock of leaving the air conditioned building. There's nothing like New York City in July. People talk about summer in St Louis or New Orleans. I haven't been to either place, but I can't believe they could get hotter than New York.

"My car's over in that lot across the street," Annie said. "Why don't you wait here? I'll just swing around and pick you up."

She walked across to the lot and stood next to her car, going through her purse for the key. In a couple of hours, by 5 a.m. or so, the street would be filled with activity because of the Fulton Fish Market a few blocks away. But right now it was deserted, except for a couple of parked cars. Annie was still fishing around in her purse. She seemed to have misplaced her keys. If she didn't hurry, I was never going to get to Higgins' place. I was getting really impatient. I stepped off the curb and began to walk across the street toward her.

Annie has always claimed that she was responsible for saving my life that night. Maybe she did; I'm not sure. I know I heard her scream a warning. I don't know whether I heard that before I heard the roar of a car's engine and saw the car parked down the street heading toward me at top speed. I'll never know which sound I reacted to first, but it doesn't matter. What does matter is that I dived back onto the sidewalk just before the car sped by—missing me by inches. It came so close that it caught the corner of my bag and ripped it away from me, leaving me holding only the strap, with nothing at the other end.

I heard tires squealing: the car made a quick U-turn and headed back for me again. Desperately I crawled for cover behind the car parked on my side of the road. Maybe he thought he'd killed me. Anyway he roared by without stopping and headed up the highway. Then there was silence. I stayed huddled beside the car. I was afraid he would come back. You could hear the waves from the East River smacking into the pier alongside the highway. A *Blade* circulation man shouted something to a driver in the garage around the corner. In the distance a subway train rumbled across the Manhattan Bridge to Brooklyn. But no other sounds. He seemed to be gone.

"Hey, hey, are you all right?"

It was Annie's voice.

"Over here," I said.

She came running up to me. Her face was pale and she was shaking.

"My God," she said. "If I hadn't looked up when I did. . ."

"I know," I said. I was trying very hard not to

panic. But this was my second brush with death in one night. How much longer would my luck hold out?

Annie looked toward the middle of the street, where the contents of my bag were spilled all over the concrete. I was still holding the strap. "He didn't hit you, did he?"

I shook my head. I was numb. Annie walked out into the street and began picking up my credit cards, my wallet and makeup. Unsteadily I went out after her and helped her. When we were finished I put the things slowly back into my bag. We went back upstairs to the city room, and I called Masters at Homicide. Nobody had to tell me the number. I knew it by heart by this time.

Chapter 13

"Why is it, Shannon," Masters asked, "that I seem to be spending most of my time these days talking to you?"

The three of us were in Dan Hodges' office. I sprawled on the sofa while Annie sat on the swivel chair behind Dan's desk. Masters walked impatiently over to the window, stared down at the lights along the East River for a few seconds and then turned back to face us. He took a cigar out of his pocket and lit it.

"I mean it used to be I could go months without ever seeing you," he said. "That was okay with me. But now I spend more time with you than I do with my wife. Why is that?"

"Just one of those lucky twists of fate, I guess."

"Okay," he said. "Let's have it. What happened?"

I told him everything I knew.

"And who's this other broad?" he said, pointing at Annie. "She a secretary or something who was working late and was going to give you a ride home?"

Annie glared at him.

"My name is Annie Klein and I am the Assistant City Editor of the New York *Blade*."

"Good for you," Masters said. He sat down on the edge of the desk and played absent-mindedly with a paperweight. His eyes looked tired, and I realized he'd been working all day and the night before. I think the case was starting to get to him.

"What's the matter, does it bother you that a woman is an editor here?" Annie asked sharply. "Maybe you think we should all be secretaries or wait on tables or scrub kitchen floors."

Masters looked pained. "Jesus, take it easy, willya? You say you're an editor, okay you're an editor. Don't go calling up NOW or Gloria Steinem on me. I get enough of that from my daughters at home."

Annie started to say something else but thought better of it.

"Now, let me see if I've got this all straight," Masters said. "Somebody tried to run you down, but you don't know who it was. They sped off in a car, but you don't know what kind. And you're pretty sure they meant to kill you, but you don't know why."

"That's about it," I told him.

He chewed thoughtfully on his cigar.

"It's a funny thing about us policemen," he said, "to solve crime we need clues. We get clues from witnesses at the scene of the crime. Now you're the only two witnesses I have to this crime. But you're not giving me any clues."

"We're trying to help the best we can," Annie said a bit testily. She was still burning about the secretary remark. "We don't know anything else."

"How about the guy inside the car? Did you see him at all? Was there just one guy or more than one? Was he big, fat, small, skinny?"

"I don't know," I said.

"What about the car? Think hard about the car."

"I don't know. I just don't know much about cars. One model looks just like another to me."

"Color?"

"Maybe green, maybe blue. But I can't be sure. It was dark."

Masters took a big puff on his cigar and blew the smoke into the air. He watched it spiral upward to the ceiling.

"You two are reporters. You're supposed to be observant, have a fine eye for detail—that sort of thing. You didn't do so good."

"Look," I said, "what is it you want me to say? That the driver was 6'2", 260 pounds, had bright red hair, a one in a million scar on his left cheek, and got away in a 1952 Studebaker with a smashed-in left headlight and license plate number AUR 783? I can't. I simply didn't see anything. I'm sorry about that too, but I can't make the facts up for you."

Masters didn't say anything.

"It was dark," Annie said, "and we were scared. And then it was all over in a few seconds."

Masters thought about all this for a while.

"Okay," he said then with a wave of his hand, "go on home. We'll contact you if we need you."

Annie and I stood up to leave. Masters walked over and opened the door. After Annie left, he took a deep breath and faced me.

"Someone tried to kill you tonight, and they came very close to succeeding," he said. "I'm not quite sure why, but I want to stop them from doing it. So be careful. The people outside will see that you get safely home in a patrol car."

He wrote down a number on a piece of paper and handed it to me.

"That's my home number," he said. "If you notice anybody or anything that seems funny to you or you think you're in danger for any reason, call me there if I'm not at the precinct. I'll have someone to help you in minutes."

I took the number and we went back out into the city room. Higgins was there waiting for me. I had called him right after the attack, and he drove down to pick me up. Masters nodded at him on his way out.

"Are you sure you're okay?" Higgins asked.

I nodded.

"Good. Let's get you out of here then,"

It was too late to write anything about the attempt on my life for the final edition now, and Hodges agreed that the best thing for me was to go home and get some sleep.

"You can write something tomorrow for

Tuesday's paper," he said. "Can you get home okay?"

"I'm fine," I told him. "I have my own personal policeman. This is Sgt Ed Higgins, one of New York's Finest."

Higgins and Hodges shook hands.

"I'm sure he'll see that you make it home safely, Lucy," Hodges said.

"I'm not so sure," I told him. "The sergeant and I have met before. I think he may be a sex maniac."

Higgins looked at me quizzically.

"Take good care of her, Sergeant," Dan said, nodding his head toward me. "Try not to let any gangster kill her. A lot of people here would be disappointed. They all want to do it themselves."

We went downstairs to Higgins' car. It turned out to be very impressive, a Porsche. I'd seen one like it once in a showroom, but I'd never ridden in one. Higgins walked around to the passenger side and opened the door for me. I looked up and down the street for any other suspicious cars, but I didn't see anything. I got inside and we headed uptown.

"Nice car," I said to him.

Higgins shrugged. "It's okay. A few years old, though. I'm thinking about getting a new one. I'm a bit of a nut about nice cars."

"Yeah," I said. "The ashtray does seem a bit dirty. Very tacky."

He glanced over at me.

"By the way," he said, "thanks a lot for that sex maniac remark back there."

"Don't worry about it," I told him. "Everyone needs some sort of hobby."

"So you really think I'm a sex maniac, huh?"

I leaned over and kissed him on the cheek.

"I'm hoping," I said.

He kissed me back.

"I have an announcement," I said. "We've got to get something to eat somewhere or I'll die. You got anything in your icebox?"

"Not much. I eat most of my meals out. Anyway, how can you have an appetite after nearly just getting killed?"

"Weird, isn't it? I was starving before it happened, though, and I'm even hungrier now. That always happens to me when I'm nervous or scared. Maybe it's all the adrenalin or something."

He looked at his watch.

"It's nearly 2:30 a.m.," he said. "I know one place that I think still has a kitchen open this late. Let's try it."

The restaurant turned out to be a snazzy sort of all-night coffee shop in the East 70's. We took a booth by the window where you could watch the traffic and people going by on First Avenue. That's one of the things that's so terrific about New York: there's always something happening.

"I think we should talk about your safety from here on in," Higgins said.

"Yeah, but before we do that, let's eat."

A waitress came over with two menus.

"What's the biggest hamburger you've got?" I asked her.

"The Superburger. It's two hamburgers in one."

"Okay, I'll take two Superburgers."

"Oh, one Superburger is pretty big, miss," the waitress said.

"Yeah, well, I'm awfully hungry. I want everything on those burgers. Lettuce, tomatoes, pickles, relish, onions, ketchup—the works. Plus an order of French fries and a large Coke."

"I'll just have some coffee," Higgins said.

I called after her to be sure and include lots of mayonnaise.

"Nobody has to shoot you or run you over," Higgins said. "They can just let you eat yourself to death."

"I'm a growing girl," I said.

"Sometime we ought to try a little more elegant dining," he said. "Maybe at a more conventional hour. I know a few places. We have time to plan."

"Maybe *you* do," I said. "My days may be numbered. I can't quite take it in yet. Everything happened so fast."

Service was pretty fast at that hour. I took a big bite out of one of the burgers. Higgins sipped his coffee thoughtfully.

"It'll be worse tomorrow," he said. "You're going to wake up and feel good—maybe, after all that food—and then you'll suddenly remember that somebody is trying to kill you. It's a kind of pressure nobody needs."

I nibbled a French fry.

"I'm not used to this in my line of work," I said. "The most dangerous thing I've ever had to worry about was a councilman who claimed I misquoted him. I'm not ready for this. How about you? You're a cop. I suppose danger is your business."

He leaned back in his chair and smiled at me. I certainly liked his smile. "There's some truth in that," he said, "but it's only business, as a rule. It's nothing personal." He leaned forward and put his hand on my arm. "We can try and help you. Don't be so stubborn."

"I don't want to live in a glass bowl, Ed," I said. "Anyway, maybe you guys will catch them. I know you won't, but maybe you will."

"Now let's be fair. You don't know the whole story. We've got some leads..."

"Oh, c'mon Ed. Masters doesn't know any more about this than I do. And I don't know anything. Of course I'm not being paid to solve cases."

He took his hand away. "That's a little tough, Lucy. It's easy to criticize the police, but let me tell you something..."

"I know, I know," I said, holding up my hand. "Next time I'm in trouble I'll call a hippie."

He threw back his head and laughed. I liked his laugh.

I ate the last crumb and then handed the check to him. "The Police Department can take care of this. That's the least they owe me for all I've gone through tonight. Now let's go."

Higgins lived in an impressive building on Riverside Drive. There was a doorman and a lobby filled with rust-coloured velvet sofas. The apartment was spacious: big living room, two bedrooms, a view of the Hudson River from glass walls. People always said you got a lot more for your money on the Upper West Side.

I put my purse on a rosewood coffee table and sank into a deep sofa.

"How about coffee?" he said.

I nodded and he disappeared into the kitchen. He came back with two big mugs of coffee on a teak tray. I took a sip.

"Hey, good coffee," I said. "Not only is he good-looking, he's domestic too."

There was a remote control for the TV on the coffee table, and he sat down next to me and switched it on. A cable channel came on. Sports scores off the United Press International wire moved slowly across the screen.

"What's the matter?" I asked him. "My conversation starting to bore you?"

"Sorry. This'll just take a second. I want to catch the late scores. There's one game I'm especially interested in."

"Football? In July? You're kidding."

"Exhibition football. Yeah, they play practically all year around now."

A score came on that said: Rams 27, Giants 6. Higgins swore softly under his breath.

"Damn," he said, "there goes fifty bucks."

"You bet on the game?" I asked.

He nodded.

"And your team lost," I said.

"Nah, I didn't bet on either team. I bet over-and-under, but I came up short. I needed 36 to win."

"You realize, of course, that I haven't got the slightest idea what you're talking about."

"Over and under is a special game where you bet on the total number of points scored. It doesn't matter which team wins, only if the total score exceeds a certain figure—in this case 36. I bet on over, which means they had to score 37 or more for me to win. They wound up at 33. Anything under 36 means I lose. If it winds up 36 on the nose, the house wins. Understand now?"

"Oh, sure," I said, "it's very clear. Do you win sometimes too?"

"Oh yeah, sometimes I win, sometimes I lose. It's like the old story about the horse player who was asked how he made out at the track. He said, 'I had a great day today—I broke even.'"

He moved closer and put his arm around me.

"You know, you've got a terrific smile," he said. "A big mouth, but a terrific smile."

I leaned over and kissed him lightly on the lips. He kissed me back. Then I slowly opened up the buttons on his shirt and began massaging his chest. He kissed me again—this time long and hard. We cuddled on the couch for a little bit and then headed for the bedroom.

When we were there, I unbuttoned his shirt the rest of the way and took it off. Then he unbuttoned my blouse. Pretty soon we were naked and under the covers. We made love slowly and for a long time. Afterward, I rolled over and lay on my side. I was facing a window wall that looked out on the river. I watched the lights from the New Jersey shoreline for a while. Then I reached down to my blouse on the floor, found a pack of cigarettes, and lit one.

"Nice view," I said.

He looked at me. "Is that all you've got to say?"

I leaned over and kissed him. "I think I like you," I said.

His hand gently touched my breast, sending shivers through me.

"Ah ha," I said, "I said you were a sex maniac."

We lay quietly in each other's arms. It had been a long, long day for me. I drifted off to sleep with my head resting on Higgins' chest and his arms around me. It felt warm and comfortable and safe. Karen Tunney's dead body, the people on South Street who tried to kill me and Tony Gianni all seemed very far away.

Chapter 14

I was back on the job at the *Blade* bright and early the next morning. Just like the postman, I thought, nothing can keep me from my appointed rounds—not snow, not sleet, not rain, not even gangsters trying to run me over with their car. The news must get through. The only trouble was I didn't know what to do next. I seemed to be at a dead end.

There's a place next door to the *Blade* with really good bagels, so I walked down and bought one along with a steaming hot cup of coffee and brought them upstairs with me. The clock in the city room said it was almost eleven. I sat down, put my feet up on my desk, and munched thoughtfully on my bagel. Someone once told me that elevating your feet helped the circulation, sending more blood to the brain. It was worth a try. Maybe if I did it long enough I'd even get an idea.

Outside it had turned into a gorgeous day—clear, in the mid 80's, with a gentle breeze blowing off the water. I watched the sailboats float by for a while. Finally I picked the morning papers off my desk and began reading everyone's coverage of the Karen Tunney murder. They didn't have anything that I didn't know about. None of the mornings had anything about the attempt on my life, because it had happened too late for deadlines. But there was something about it in the afternoon *Post*. The headline said, "Hit-And-Run-Terror for Kimberly Case Reporter." There was an interview with Masters:

> Lt. Masters said Miss Shannon had provided him with some key details about the driver of the car who tried to run her down. He was hopeful of a break in the case very soon. "I can't disclose Miss Shannon's information," he said. "But we're getting closer to some answers in this case. I think we'll be making some arrests shortly."

Oh, sure, I muttered, sure you do. Pressure must be getting intense if Masters was trying so hard to make it look like the Department knew something.

I went through the rest of the paper without much interest. Nothing much else was happening in the world. Everyone was on vacation. Diane von Furstenberg was sunning on the French Riviera. Caroline Kennedy was on Cape Cod, although she thought she might hop over to Europe for a few days. Elizabeth Taylor had thrown a terrific barbecue the other night at a house she was renting in California: the guests dined on rack of lamb, lobster and corn on the cob. I still felt hungry after I finished my bagel, so I wandered out into the hall to buy a bag of salted peanuts from the vending machine.

The glamorous life of big-time journalism.

I came back and put my feet up again. Nose to the grindstone, shoulder to the wheel. Horatio Alger would have been proud of me. The telephone rang. It was Barlow calling from the other side of the city room. God, that drove me crazy.

"You've got to do something about this telephone compulsion of yours," I said to him. "From this it's only a short step to making obscene calls to teenaged babysitters."

"You know you have to write an article for tomorrow's paper about the car incident? The sooner you get it finished the better."

"I know about it," I said.

"Are you planning anything else for today?"

"I've got a few leads I want to follow up."

"You want to tell me about them?"

"No," I said. "Not particularly. Look, Walter, I really think it would be a lot better if you would just let me operate on my own on this story. It's my life on the line here, right? So I think you owe me at least the courtesy of allowing me to handle things the way I want to. I'll let you know if anything important turns up."

He muttered something and hung up.

So now what? I really had no leads. I didn't have the slightest idea of where to go from there.

I lit a cigarette and tried to think. What facts did I have? Nancy Kimberly was dead. That was a fact. John Luckman was dead. That was another fact. Karen Tunney was dead. Fact number three. Now what about Janet Langmann? Probably dead. But not a fact. Body never found. Was that significant? If she was alive, where was she? She was an unknown factor.

And of course there was another question. *Why* were they dead? They all worked at Stereo Heaven, so obviously Stereo Heaven was a factor. Gianni said Nancy had something he wanted. So maybe the others at the store knew about it too. What could it be? The only lead I had was the briefcase Karen had mentioned.

And the other question. Who killed them? Tony Gianni was my only choice so far. Who else could it be? Who in this affair was left alive? Was Janet Langmann a suspect? I supposed she was, as long as she remained unaccounted for, but that was pretty far-fetched. Of course there could be someone I didn't know about. Who was the woman who lost the briefcase, for instance? Or was something else going on at Stereo Heaven that had nothing to do with Gianni?

But one thing I did know for sure. I was really tired of waiting around for someone to attack me. I decided I had to make something happen.

Gianni Sand and Gravel Co. was listed in the Brooklyn phone book. I dialed the number and asked for the man himself.

"He's tied up in a meeting," a woman's voice said. "Can I take a message?"

"Tell him Lucy Shannon of the *Blade* wants to talk to him. Tell him it's important. Tell him if he doesn't want to come to the phone, then I'll come out there with a couple of photographers and reporters to do a major photo essay for the *Blade* on the mob influence on our waterfront. Tell him that, will you?"

The woman put me on hold. A few minutes later, Gianni came on the line.

"Miss Shannon," he said. "How are you today?"

"Not too bad considering someone tried to run me over last night. They just missed."

"I heard about that on the news. That was too bad."

"Too bad that they tried or too bad that they missed?"

Gianni chuckled softly. "I see you're still under the illusion that I want to harm you. I'm just a simple business man trying to do an honest..."

"Cut the crap, Gianni. I want to see you. In person. As soon as possible."

"What about?"

"Well, it's not about sand and gravel. I'll tell you when I see you. What's your answer?"

"All right," he said. "How about tomorrow afternoon?"

"Tomorrow's fine."

"Shall we say right here in my office at 2:30?"

"We shall," I said. "And one point I think I

should make. Both the police and my newspaper know exactly where I'm going. So don't go getting any funny ideas about trying anything. It might be a little obvious. Even you wouldn't be able to beat the rap for something like that."

"Thanks for the advice. See you tomorrow afternoon."

I hung up and walked into Hodges' office. He was working at his desk and didn't look up. I went to the liquor cabinet against the wall, poured myself a stiff Scotch and dropped two ice cubes in it.

I fell into the chair facing his desk and took a big drink.

"I'm seeing Gianni tomorrow."

"You're what?"

"I'm going to see Gianni tomorrow in Brooklyn at his Sand and Gravel Works. I feel like I've got to do something. I can't keep hanging around like this waiting for something to happen. This is the only way I can think of to maybe get some answers."

"Is it the only way you can think of to maybe wind up dead?"

"Gianni's too smart to do something like that," I said.

But what if I had an "accident"? He was smart enough for that too.

"You got any bright ideas about what I should do today?" I said. "Any loose ends that come to mind, something you want me to check?"

Hodges thought for a minute. Then he leaned forward in his chair and snapped his fingers.

"How about the parents? Nancy Kimberly's parents. No one's talked to them yet that I know of."

"That's right," I said. "They were out of the country and unreachable when the murder happened. We kept checking for a few days, and then I guess we forgot about it. I haven't read anywhere about anyone ever talking to them."

"Well, that's one loose end," Dan said. "And then there's Janet Langmann."

"She's definitely a loose end," I said.

I went back into the city room and found a New Jersey phone book. There was no listing for the Kimberlys. Then I remembered—they had an unlisted number. I'd have to drive out there again. Maybe tomorrow, I thought, after I talk to Gianni.

I walked down to the library and checked out the envelope containing the articles that had been written about Janet Langmann. Her family lived in Kew Gardens. I found the number in the Queens book and called. A man answered.

"Mr Langmann?" I asked. "My name is Lucy Shannon, I'm a reporter for the *Blade*. I wonder if I could come out now and talk to you."

"We have nothing to say," he said. "I keep telling you people we have nothing to say."

I decided to try the personal approach.

"Look, please don't think I'm just another reporter bothering you. I have a personal involvement in this case, and in your daughter's safety. Maybe your wife mentioned me to you. I was with her at Janet's apartment when she called the police... I told her to call the police. And I've been threatened myself--"

"We want to be alone now," he said. "We don't want to be bothered."

He hung up. So much for the personal approach.

I thought about it for a while. It's easy to say no over the phone. Sometimes, if you show up on their doorstep, notebook in hand, people change their minds. Anyway it was worth a try.

Kew Gardens is a forty-minute subway ride from the *Blade* building. I took the IRT uptown, picked up the E line at 53rd Street and rode to Queens Boulevard. The Langmanns lived in a modest bungalow a five minute walk from the train. The street was nice and quiet, lined with trees, like Nancy Kimberly's street.

I rang the bell and waited. Would Mr Langmann yell at me through the door? Would he open it and slam it in my face? It would be nice to have a job where people were happy to see you when you came calling.

Mrs Langmann opened the door.

"Hi," I said. I quickly shoved part of my shoulder inside the door. "Remember me? Lucy Shannon from the *Blade*?"

"Oh... yes..." She relaxed her grip on the door and I edged inside before she had a chance to change her mind.

"I just want to talk to you and your husband for a few minutes... I know you're under a strain..."

She was walking slowly into the living room and

I followed her. Mr Langmann was sitting in an easy chair, with the day's newspapers around him on the floor. Even though he was sitting down, he still looked big, a muscular man in his fifties, with a bit of a beer belly straining his white T-shirt.

"This is Miss Shannon, Tom," his wife said. "You remember I mentioned her? Won't you sit down?" she said to me.

Mr Langmann was glaring at me but he made no move to throw me out.

"So tell me," I said, "has there been anything new at all?"

This kind of probing, incisive journalism is my specialty.

"No," she said, "nothing at all."

Then silence. The ball was back in my court.

"How have you been spending the time waiting for some word about your daughter?"

"We just sit here every day waiting. I want to hear something, but at the same time I don't. As long as nobody finds her body, there's still a glimmer of hope. Not much. But it's all that keeps me going."

She was talking more now. I quietly slipped my tape recorder out of my handbag and laid it on the coffee table in front of me. I pressed down the record button. No one stopped me.

"Tell me about your daughter," I said.

"She was a wonderful girl, Miss Shannon, a wonderful girl. Everyone who knew her loved her."

I wondered if she realized she was talking about her daughter in the past tense.

"She was only working at that terrible store to

make money so we didn't have to pay so much for her college education. We're not poor, but Tom hasn't been able to work much in the past year. He has a heart condition."

He still didn't say anything.

"Anyway, Janet thought she could help out by taking the job. She was going to NYU full-time, majoring in education. She was going to be a teacher. She said she wanted to do something to help people."

Mr Langmann leaned forward in his chair and spoke for the first time. "Do you think this guy Gianni killed my daughter?"

"I don't know," I said. "We're all hoping she's not dead."

"But if she is, do you think Gianni's responsible?"

"He seems to be the only likely suspect the police have at this point," I said.

"Well, I want you to tell him something for me, if you ever see him again." He slowly clenched and unclenched his fists. "Tell him that if he killed my Janet, I'm going to kill him. With my own bare hands. I'm not afraid of him or his goons. I'm not afraid of anybody. They can't kill my baby and get away with it. Tell him that, will you?"

An uneasy silence hung in the room. I stared down at the table and watched the tape recorder wheels whirring silently.

Langmann shrugged his shoulders.

"Okay," he said, "have you got what you came for? I told you not to come here, but you came anyway. So why don't you just go now and write your article? I hope you sell a lot of papers."

"Mr. Langmann..."

He leaned forward, looking at me with tears in his eyes. "The thing you have to understand," he said, "is that Janet never hurt anyone. She never caused anyone a bit of trouble in her whole damn life. Do you understand what I'm saying? So why did they kill her? Why? That's the thing I'll never understand. She couldn't have been involved with them. The other girl I could see getting into trouble. But not Janet. Never Janet."

"When you say the other girl, do you mean Nancy Kimberly?"

"Yes. That one."

"Did you ever meet her?"

"Two or three times."

"And you didn't like her?"

"Let's just say we didn't think Janet should be around her," his wife said. "She was a mover, a schemer, always looking out for herself. Very self-centered. And there was this feeling I always had about her—that she was headed for some sort of bad trouble. I didn't want Janet to go around with her."

That was the same description of Nancy that Mrs Feinstein had given me. Someone who looked like she was headed for trouble.

"Oh, she was a pretty little thing, I'll grant you," Langmann said. "A real looker, if you like that type. Auburn hair, big brown eyes, a face like a movie star. And she always wore the kind of clothes that would show off her figure. She used her looks to get what she wanted.

"No, I didn't like her. And I can't help blaming her for what happened to Janet. I think she did something that got them both killed."

He got up and put his arm around his wife. They were both weeping.

When I got back to the office, I tried to concentrate on the article I was writing. Somehow I got it finished by deadline, but my mind wasn't really on it. Maybe the emotional scene with the Langmanns had really gotten to me. Or maybe it was just nerves over my appointment with Gianni tomorrow. But I couldn't shake this strange feeling that there was a clue that I was overlooking—a clue that might make some sense out of this whole crazy mess.

Chapter 15

It was a little after six by the time I got back to my apartment. There was no one waiting there to greet me with slippers and a cold drink. No one gave me a welcome home kiss. No one asked me if I'd had a nice day at the office. Just the same as it was last week and the week before that. I wondered what it would be like to come home and be met by a husband, a couple of kids and a barking dog. Maybe I should try it sometime.

I poured myself a Scotch and took it into the living room. I sat there, sipping and thinking about my meeting with Gianni tomorrow. I was getting more and more worried about it. Why had I set it up anyway? I had no real idea of what I was trying to accomplish. The whole idea began to seem crazier and crazier.

What I needed to do was to talk to someone and stop sitting here in this lonely apartment feeling depressed. I picked up the phone and dialed Higgins' number. There was no answer. I tried the precinct, but they said he was working on a case. I left a message asking him to call.

Next I tried Annie Klein.

"Let's make this brief, huh, Lucy?" she said.

"Are you busy?"

"That's just the point—I'm not busy for the first time in weeks. Every night recently it's seemed like either I had to work late or Don was tied up at the office or on the road. We hardly even saw each other. So we set tonight aside just to be with each other. A nice quiet romantic dinner. Candles, champagne, the whole works. So make it snappy, or you'll ruin the mood."

"Well, actually I was going to ask you if you'd mind inviting me over to dinner tonight."

There was a long pause on the other end.

"Is that a yes or no?" I asked.

"Maybe you didn't hear what I said. Don and I are planning to have a quiet, romantic candlelight dinner tonight. I don't know quite how to tell you this, Lucy, but my idea of a romantic dinner doesn't include you as one of the diners."

"You'd hardly even know I was there," I said. "I won't say a word until the dessert. Honest, this is kind of important, Annie. You know me, I hardly ever ask you for a favor."

"Let me put it this way, Lucy: No."

"I see."

"What's the matter with you, anyway? You're really acting crazy—even for you."

"I guess I'm a little nervous," I said. "Actually, I'm a lot nervous,"

I told her about the meeting with Gianni tomorrow.

"Yeah, I can see where that might make a person edgy," Annie said.

I said it sure could.

"Okay," she sighed finally, "we're having dinner about 7:30 or so. If you want to come over afterward for a few minutes for a drink, I'll explain it to Don somehow."

"Thanks," I said. "I'm going to try a few other things first. But if they don't work out, maybe I'll take you up on it."

After I hung up, I dialed the number for my answering service. They said I'd gotten a call about an hour earlier from someone named Tom Donnelly. Tom Donnelly. I'd forgotten about him in all the excitement. Maybe that was the answer. I dialed his number, but there was no answer. Just like everybody else in New York City tonight, he seemed to have something to do.

I walked over to the living room window, finished my drink and looked down at Third Avenue. It was a beautiful summer night, and the street was crowded. Lots of people walked by, holding hands. Almost everyone seemed to be with someone except me. I needed badly to talk to someone. I also needed another drink.

The bottle of Scotch was in the kitchen, so I went in there and refilled my glass. I sat down at the table and felt very sorry for myself. It's hard not to feel sorry for yourself when you're a 33-year-old woman who has nothing better to do than sit alone in her kitchen and drink Scotch. Finally I grabbed my handbag and headed for the door. I just had to get outside. Maybe I'd try to find Donnelly.

The best place to try first was Elaine's. Donnelly told me he spent virtually every night there when he was in town during the summer. If he wasn't there or if he was there with some other woman, that was okay too. I wasn't doing anything else anyway, and the ride up there would kill some time.

When I got there, Donnelly didn't seem to be around, so I walked over to the bar and ordered a drink. One of the nice things about a place like Elaine's is that a woman drinking alone at the bar doesn't get hassled. All kinds of single aspiring starlets are milling around so one lone woman doesn't seem so enticing a target. I sat there for about forty minutes sipping Scotch. No one bothered me, no one talked to me. I amused myself by trying to see how many celebrities I could count in the place. I was up to twenty-nine when Donnelly walked in.

He was with a half dozen people, a couple that I knew from the other night and a few I'd never seen before. None of them looked like a date, so I decided it was okay to make my move. Elaine greeted them effusively and led them to a big table against the wall.

Gloria Steinem would be proud of me, I thought to myself as I walked over to greet him.

"Lucy! What are you doing here?"

"Looking for you, actually."

"Well, I'm glad you found me. Sit down. This is Lucy Shannon, my favorite police reporter. Do you know everyone? Here, let me introduce you."

Everyone wanted to know all about my escapades. They listened attentively while I talked about finding Karen Tunney's body. Then they oohed-and-aahed when I told them about nearly being run over in front of the *Blade*. I could tell I was a big hit. I started to feel a little better.

Donnelly leaned over and hugged me. "God," he said, "to think all this happened to you since I talked to you yesterday morning. Now if you'd come out to the Island with me you would have had a quiet weekend with nobody trying to kill you. Of course," he added, "you would have missed out on all that excitement."

"Tom," I said, in a low voice, "could I talk to you for a minute? Sort of alone. I want to ask you something."

"Sure," he said. "Let's take a walk."

We excused ourselves and went outside. We walked up Second Avenue. Traffic was jammed up behind a taxi stalled in the middle of the street. Everyone was leaning on his horn.

"I just need to talk," I said. "I'm really scared."

I told him about it.

He put his arm around my shoulders.

"What can I do to help?" he said.

"Could you keep me company tonight?" I asked. "I'll be all right if I'm with a lot of people. And... I think... you're pretty patient and understanding."

He leaned over and kissed me.

"That's settled," he said. "Now let's go back. You could probably use another drink."

We stayed at Elaine's for a couple of hours. I got

pretty zonked. I don't remember a whole lot that went on. Eventually I said I thought I should go home. Donnelly wanted to know if I was all right.

"More or less," I said. I tried standing up and almost fell on my face.

"This will shock you," I said to him. "But I think I may have had too much to drink. I know it's hard to believe. I always hold my liquor."

"I'll take you home," he said.

We caught a cab and headed downtown.

"I don't know exactly how to bring this up delicately," I said, "but I think it's only fair to tell you that I'm not exactly in shape tonight to set any new sex records."

"I agree. Why don't I just say goodnight to you at your door?"

"You don't mind?"

"It's fine. You've got a big day ahead of you tomorrow. Get some sleep."

The cab pulled up in front of my building. Donnelly reached over and kissed me.

"You be careful tomorrow," he said. "And call me afterward and tell me what happened. If I'm not home, you can get me at the studio."

"Okay, I will."

"Promise? I'll be waiting."

"Promise."

I kissed him again and then went upstairs. Every part of my body felt awful. I went into the bedroom and got undressed. The clock on my night table said 3:15 a.m. I decided to forget about brushing my teeth or washing my face and just collapsed on the bed. I was almost asleep when the phone rang.

"City desk," I said sleepily. "Scoops bought and sold cheap."

"This is Ed. I've been trying to get you all night."

"I've been out trying to forget what I have to do tomorrow. It almost worked. I have a date with Tony Gianni."

Higgins let out a low whistle of surprise.

"But he tried to kill you, Lucy."

"So, no one's perfect. Don't get the idea that he was slavering to get his hands on me. I had to do some fast talking to get past his secretary, but I did it. I told him I was telling you and the paper about it in case anything happened to me. So I don't see why I should be nervous."

"I don't know," he said. "I don't like it."

"Do you think I do? But I had to do something. Listen, I've got to get some sleep. I'll talk to you about it afterward, okay?"

"Sure. Boy, you are really something." He gave a low laugh. "I don't know too many women—or men either—who'd have the nerve to talk their way into Tony Gianni's office by threatening to write an exposé about him. I hope you know what you're doing."

"So do I," I said.

I hung up and walked slowly back to bed. I wasn't sleepy any more. I felt shaken up. Higgins was right: I had talked myself into Gianni's office by threatening to write an exposé about him. Only I had never told that to Ed. I had never told anyone, except Gianni's secretary and, probably through her, Gianni himself. So how did Ed find out about it? I lay there for a long time, thinking, until I drifted off into an uneasy sleep.

Chapter 16

Gianni's Sand and Gravel Co. was a pleasant red brick building located just off the Shore Parkway in Brooklyn, overlooking the waters of Gravesend Bay. A sprinkler sparkled under the afternoon sun as it whipped back and forth over the neat lawn. A sign on the front door said to ring for admittance.

A pretty young woman in her twenties answered the door. She had dark hair cut stylishly short and was wearing a chic red cotton suit. She wasn't carrying a Tommy gun or holding a hand grenade in her teeth. So far, so good.

I identified myself and she led me into a reception area with modern furniture. A Beatles song was coming out of the stereo system. I sat down while she went to announce me. A blond coffee table was piled with magazines. *Time, Newsweek, Readers' Digest, People.* The place reminded me of my dentist's office. Organized crime was very organized these days.

The secretary came back and ushered me into his

office. Gianni was sitting behind a big blond wood desk in an acre of shag carpeting. Behind him was a window overlooking the Bay. On either side of him stood Rocky and Les, looking impassive.

"This is a great layout," I said. "There must be a lot of money in sand and gravel."

"It's a living," Gianni said.

"Who are those two guys," I said, pointing with my chin to Rocky and Les, "your liaisons with the Better Business Bureau?"

"Fuck you," Les said.

"These two gentlemen provide valuable assistance to my company in a variety of ways," Gianni said.

"How about if they leave?"

"What?"

"How about if they leave? You know. Go bye-bye. I know they're both wonderful human beings, and it's no reflection on them, but I would feel more comfortable if they weren't here. What I want to talk about is just between the two of us."

"The hell with that," Rocky said.

"Why don't you boys take a little walk?" Gianni said.

"You better get her frisked, boss," Les said. "She's nuts."

"She's wired," Rocky said.

"Take a walk," Gianni said. "I said take a walk."

They trailed out, with much head-shaking and protesting.

"I want to make a deal," I said, when we were alone. "I think you and I should work together. You tell me everything you know about Nancy Kimberly and I'll tell you everything I know. You asked me before, now I'm willing. How does that sound?"

He took a cigar from a dark-wood humidor on his desk, unwrapped it and lit it slowly.

"You haven't got anything to give me," he said.

"I know that. That's why I haven't talked to you since that night at Antonio's. So what's the point in me talking to you? How can you deal? You got nothing to deal."

I took a deep breath and plunged ahead.

"Let me put it this way. It looks like you've got a very nice little operation going here. On the outside, it's legitimate. Nobody really hassles you—not the cops, not the feds, and not the politicians. You make like an honest businessman, they don't look into your dealings and everyone's happy. Right?"

He puffed on his cigar.

"Now the point is," I said, "I can change all that. I can make things very, very hot for you, Tony. If I were to get a *Blade* investigation going on you—detailing all your shoddy dealings and demanding that the authorities look into them—things would start to happen. There'd be tremendous public pressure on them to do something. That's the power of the press. And I don't think the other mob leaders around town would be too happy with you either. They don't like that kind of publicity. If you took a fall, they could be in trouble, too. In fact, they might be so worried about it they'd decide it was better to bump you off before the investigation dug too deeply."

Gianni's face was expressionless.

"So that's your deal?" he asked.

"That's my deal. If you don't help me, then I put you and your operation under the public spotlight. If you work with me, I forget about it. There's no *Blade* investigation. And besides that, I'll owe you a big favor. You never know when you might need a friend in the press."

He swiveled his chair around and sat with his back to me, looking out of the window. After a while he swiveled around again.

"You're really something, kid," he said softly. "Really something. You got brains, you got guts, and you got looks. Not looks that mean anything to me, but looks anyway. You could really go far in the right business. A crummy newspaper reporter. You're wasting your life."

"Some of us consider it a noble profession," I said.

"How much you earn? In a year?"

"Last year, thirty-one thousand. Including overtime."

"Thirty-one thousand. That's a joke. I can earn that in five minutes."

He sat back in his chair and sighed.

"All right," he said. He put his cigar in a big glass ashtray. "You want to know about Nancy Kimberly, I'll tell you about Nancy Kimberly. About six weeks ago, I lost something. Somebody in my employ made a mistake. She was supposed to deliver something and she stopped off somewhere and the package got mislaid."

He paused for effect.

"She stopped off at Stereo Heaven," he said.

"Surprise, surprise," I said.

"She said the record store was her only stop. So we went there and asked them nicely if they had seen the case. No one there knew anything."

"What about the girl who lost it?" I asked suddenly.

He looked at me blankly. "She is no longer in our employ."

There was a short pause.

"We started watching the store," he said. "We noticed the Kimberly girl was spending a lot of money. So we went back and we talked to them again. We tried very hard to get our point across to these people. I don't think we were unreasonable. We gave them seventy-two hours to get it together for us. Still no dice."

"And that's when you killed Nancy Kimberly," I said.

"You said that, I didn't. We haven't killed anybody. Yet."

Something I had heard yesterday suddenly popped into my head. It all made more sense now.

"What was in the briefcase?"

He blew smoke toward the ceiling. "Five hundred thousand dollars," he said, "give and take a little."

"That's a lot of money."

"It's chicken feed," Gianni said. "In my business,

it's chicken feed. What the hell."

"Then why—?"

"Listen sweetheart, I need respect in this business. It's part of the image. It's important. Me and my people, we have to have respect. Word goes out some jerk took half a million from me and I wrote it off, right? So people figure, Gianni lost it. You see? I need the money or somebody has got to pay something, some way."

"But wait a minute," I said. "If you don't care about the money, if all you want is to make an example of somebody, why are you still involved in this? Nancy Kimberly's dead—everybody who worked at Stereo Heaven is dead. You obviously made your point. So why are you searching Janet Langmann's apartment and picking me up off the street to ask me questions and following me—"

"Well, just see if you can figure that out, honey."

"But they're all dead," I said. "So why do you care anymore?"

"Oh, we care," he said. "We care a lot."

I tried to figure it out.

"Let's drop this," Gianni said. "Why don't we talk about you? You could make a lot of money, do you know that? Why don't you come to work for me?"

"That's a great idea," I said. "What do you think I'd be good at? Selling heroin in school playgrounds?"

Gianni's face was impassive. "You wouldn't have to quit your job," he said. "You could keep it."

"Well thanks," I said, "but I think I'll stick to the

one job. It doesn't pay very well. But, and please don't take this personally, it has integrity."

He burst out laughing suddenly. I jumped. "Integrity," he said. "That's good." He went on laughing for a while. "Integrity," he said. He took out another cigar. "I'm sorry," he said. "I only offered because I understood you didn't care for your job too much. The way I heard it you thought every day about some new line of work you could try. I was only trying to help you out."

A chill went through me.

"Who told you that?" I said sharply.

"What?"

"You said every day I thought about some new line of work. Where did you hear that?"

Gianni raised his eyebrows. "I hear things," he said. "I hear a lot of things. From a lot of people."

I stood up.

"Thanks for seeing me," I said, "and thanks for your help. I would like to ask you one more question before I go, if you don't mind."

"Go ahead."

"Did you try to kill me the other night?"

He stood up too, and looked directly into my eyes.

"No," he said.

"That's the truth?"

"That's the truth."

Slowly I walked outside and over to my car. It was parked near a hydrant and one of New York's Finest, dogged in his pursuit of crime, had put a ticket on it. Irony, I thought. Gianni sits inside the building in a plush office making million dollar crooked deals and nobody lays a glove on him. I park my broken-down car outside, and they nail me. I tore up the ticket and threw it away. Then I got in the car and drove back to Manhattan.

Chapter 17

I walked straight into the office and picked up the phone. Annie and Barlow both looked up at me expectantly. I waved to them and called the Medical Examiner's office to check something out. They both came up to me as I was hanging up.

"Well?" Annie said. "How'd it go?"

"It went," I said.

"The interview with Gianni?"

"Yeah. It went. I'll tell you all about it later. What time is it?"

"About four-thirty," Barlow said. "Why? You going someplace?"

"I want to run out to Teaneck. See if the Kimberlys are back. I won't be gone more than a couple of hours."

Annie shrugged and went back to her desk. Barlow grabbed my arm and steered me to a quiet corner.

"Is everything okay?" he asked. "Are you all right?"

"No really," I said. "Everything's cool."

"You've got to remember that these people mean business. You've got to be careful. Don't get yourself killed."

"Why Walter," I said, with genuine surprise, "I didn't know you cared."

Probably I should have told him what Gianni had said to me, and my theory about it all. But I had the feeling that the case was close to breaking wide open and I wanted to be the one who did it. I wasn't exactly sure how to go about it. I thought maybe I'd find some answers at the Kimberly place. I drove up the East River Drive, across the George Washington Bridge and into New Jersey. The bridge was clogged with rush hour traffic, so it was near six before I got there. I parked the car on the street and walked up the drive.

The house looked dark and deserted. A couple of weeks worth of mail sat uncollected in the mailbox. I wandered around to the back and tried the door there. It was locked. I thought for a while about the penalty for breaking and entering. Then I walked into the yard and found a big rock. I picked it up, covered my eyes and smashed one of the glass panes on the door with it. Then I reached through the opening, unlocked the door, and let myself in.

Someone had beaten me to it. Drawers pulled out, furniture cut up, everything strewn all over the floor. It looked just like Janet Langmann's place. Bedroom, kitchen, dining room—they all looked the same. Everything was dusty. Whoever had done this was long gone.

One for the Money 173

There wasn't much point in my going through all the stuff. If there was anything here worth finding, they'd have taken it with them. I shoved some papers off one of the chairs and sat down. Jesus, I was getting tired of all this. Everytime I turned around I was running into murder victims, gangsters, and ransacked houses. What I felt like doing was covering a nice, boring City Council beat for a while. I stared out the window. It was starting to get dark, it looked like rain. I decided to drive back to the office, call Masters, and tell him everything I knew.

Outside, the first drops of rain were already coming down. I sprinted for my car. I flicked on the wipers, and was just about to pull away from the curb when I noticed the car sitting in the driveway of the house next door, where Charlie Allen lived, the guy who invited me in for a drink the day I'd come up here after Nancy Kimberly's body was found. It was a green Ford with New Jersey plates. I had seen that car once before. It had tried to run me down in front of the *Blade* building.

Now I'll be the first to admit that some of the things I'd done so far that day weren't terribly bright. Going to see Gianni by myself was dumb. So was breaking into the Kimberly house. And so was not going to the authorities right away with everything I knew. But what I did next was the dumbest of all. I got out of the car, walked around to the back of Charlie Allen's house, and rang the bell. There was no answer. Then I picked up another rock and put it through the window.

I saw the gun the minute I got into the house. The woman holding it had a face like a movie star, long auburn hair parted down the middle, and big brown eyes. The gun was a .38 caliber pistol, and she was pointing it right at me.

"Hello, Nancy," I said.

Chapter 18

Nancy Kimberly stared impassively at me from behind the gun.

"Fuck you," she said.

"Now, is that a nice way to talk to me? Didn't you read all those nice things I wrote about you? I made you a star, kid."

"You screwed it up, Shannon," she said. "You really screwed it up."

"You're the one who screwed it up," I said.

She pointed the gun briefly toward the living room. "Go in there and sit down."

I went in and sat down on the couch. It was a pleasant, comfortable room with thick red carpeting and maple furniture. An old clock on the mantel ticked loudly. On a round table next to me was a picture of Charlie Allen and what must be his wife.

"How about some coffee?" I said. "And where's Charlie?"

She stood facing me. The gun didn't waver.

"Don't look so grim," I said. "Think of how happy everyone is going to be when they find out you're still alive—our readers, the police, the neighbours, Tony Gianni.... I'm happy myself, but I already knew about it today before I saw you. I called the Medical Examiner's office just to make sure. They said the corpse in your apartment had blue eyes. Janet Langmann's father said you had brown eyes. And you do."

"Poor Janet," Nancy said. "She just happened to be in the wrong place at the wrong time. She was at my apartment when they came, and they thought she was me. That's why they killed her. The mob."

"Right," I said. "Because of the money."

She got up and walked over to the front window. She was still carrying the gun. "You came alone," she said.

"That's right."

"Kind of a dumb thing to do." She came back and sat down in a chintz wing chair opposite me.

"You're telling me," I said.

"See, they came to see me at the store," Nancy said. "They weren't really nasty, you know, but they said they wanted that money back. They just guessed we had it, how could they know we had it?"

Her tone was reasonable and friendly, but somehow I found that gun very distracting. I guess I have this little idiosyncrasy: I get nervous when someone is holding a loaded .38 on me. Maybe I need therapy.

"So I told them I didn't know anything about it,

and they went away. But they came back. They started making threats."

She fell into a brooding silence.

I cleared my throat. "So what did you do then?" I asked.

"I told them to fuck off," she said. "Hell, it wasn't their money anyway. A bunch of hoods. They probably stole it from somebody. I had as much right to it as they did." She looked at me. "Don't you think so?"

"Oh, sure," I said.

"And anyway, by the time they came back, I spent some of it. I didn't have it all any more. I moved, I bought clothes." She gazed in the general direction of my right ear. "A once in a lifetime break," she said softly.

"You weren't afraid of them," I said.

"I figured he was bluffing," she said. "Anyway, you have to take risks in this life. You can't get anywhere without taking risks." She began to laugh. "I don't have to tell you that," she said. "You take risks all the time."

She went on laughing for quite a while. I managed to work up a sick smile.

"I told John that," she said. "That slob. Can you imagine? He wanted to give it back. We had a 50-50 split and he wanted to give it back. All of it. He wanted to give them mine too. He even wanted to pay back what was spent. Boy, what a baby."

The clock on the mantel ticked loudly.

"You know, I really wish you'd put that gun

away," I said. "It makes me nervous."

"We had a big fight about it," she said. "I couldn't get him to think straight. He wanted to talk to them." She paused. "But then, see, they killed him. I went over there to get him to change his mind and I found him dead."

"What a bummer," I said. "So you knew they weren't kidding."

"Yeah, right. So I knew I had to split so I rushed back to my place to get some things and Janet was there. She had my key and I guess she went up there to pick up some stuff for the store or something. So they thought she was me." She leaned toward me intently. "See, I knew that was what happened. She was dead and they thought she was me. So I thought if they thought they killed me, they wouldn't look for me, right?"

"They must have been pretty mad," I said. "Smashing her up like that."

"Yeah," she said.

"And your parents were away. So nobody was around to know you were alive."

"Right. Terrific timing," she said. "Everybody thought it was me."

"But you were going to tell them eventually that you were alive," I said.

"Who?"

"Your parents."

"Oh," she said. "Sure. Right."

The clock began to chime. Seven o'clock. I wondered how long it would take for Barlow and Annie to wonder where I was.

"Gosh," I said. "I better call my office. I always check in. Phone in the kitchen?" I started to get up.

"Sit down," she said. "Don't you want to hear the rest of the story?"

"Oh, I think I can guess," I said casually. "You hid out in your folks' place. That makes sense."

I thought about my first visit there. She was probably inside the house, a few feet away from me.

"Yeah, and those goons showed up. I got out before they saw me and came over here. Charlie's out on the West coast." She frowned. "That creep. He was always watching me. I think he's some kind of pervert. My mother almost called the cops about him."

I think we both thought about the car at the same time. Charlie's car. The one she tried to kill me with.

"That's the whole story," she said. Her eyes looked like steel balls. "You're the only one who knows it."

"Where's the money?" I asked, trying to continue the chat. The atmosphere had changed.

"I'm the only one who knows that," she said. "You ask too many questions. You're nosy. You could get hurt."

She stood up. "Let's go," she said.

I didn't move. "Go where?"

"I said, let's *go*," she said.

"You know," I said desperately, "you didn't fool Gianni. He knows you're alive. I saw him yesterday. He's looking for you."

"The hell he is," she said.

"He is," I said. I got up slowly. "He told me. Yesterday."

"Well, Gianni won't talk," Nancy said. "And you will. So let's go. We'll take a little drive. In your car. You drive."

I saw the scenario clearly. An accident. And one dead reporter. Such a shame. A girl with a bright future.

We went outside and she closed the door carefully behind us. I saw a Porsche parked next to my car on the street. He must have followed me.

I stopped so suddenly that she walked into me. I felt the gun in my back. "Look out!" I screamed, pointing wildly toward her house. "Over there!"

She was caught off balance. I gave her a hard shove and took off across the lawn toward a thick hedge in the next yard. It was the closest cover.

She yelled something and fired two shots. Something smacked into the soft ground behind me. I threw a quick glance back and saw her taking dead aim. I tripped over something and fell headlong just as she fired again. There was another shot, but I didn't feel anything.

I opened my eyes, which I had squeezed tight shut, and looked back. She was lying on her face on the ground behind me. Higgins was still crouched next to the Porsche in a firing position with his gun in both hands. He stood up slowly.

I got up too with some difficulty. I was shaking from head to foot.

We both stood over her body. The gun was lying

near her right hand. There was a red splotch on the back of her blouse. Higgins kicked the gun away from her and bent down to feel her pulse.

Up and down the street porch lights were snapping on, and screen doors were slamming. Neighbors were coming out to see what the noise was about. In the distance police sirens were wailing.

Chapter 19

The Teaneck cops handled it first. They took us back to their headquarters, in one of those red brick, antiseptic-looking municipal suburban complexes. The town's library was on one side, a hospital across the street. We sat on formica chairs in an air-conditioned cubicle and drank coffee while I tried to explain everything I knew. Pretty soon the New York cops got there and took things over. Then the press began descending in droves.

I got one big break. A New Jersey cop was friendly enough to let me slip away early and call my office. That gave me time before all the long questioning began to talk to a rewriteman, and the *Blade* was on the street with it before the other reporters even showed up. Otherwise, I might have wound up getting scooped on my own story.

Masters was one of the first New York cops there. For a guy who'd just gotten all the answers to a baffling mass murder case, he didn't seem too happy.

"I suppose you're pretty proud of yourself, Shannon," he said. "Maybe you think the department ought to give you a special commendation or something, huh?"

I was beginning to get this vague feeling his unhappiness had something to do with me. Call it woman's intuition.

"A simple thank you will suffice," I said.

"What I ought to do is lock you up and throw away the key."

"Lock *me* up? Why? What's the charge?"

"For openers, we could try withholding evidence. Then maybe a couple of counts of breaking and entering. And I'm sure there's a lot more if we put our minds to it."

I didn't say anything.

"You know that press pass you're carrying doesn't give you the right to be a one woman police force. You get evidence, you find anything out— you're supposed to come to me with it. Not go running off half-cocked on your own. You think I like finding out that my case has been solved from some cop in New Jersey? And now you want me to thank you. What kind of jerk do you think I am anyway?"

The snappy comeback here would be: "I don't know, how many kinds are there?" But I was tired of snappy comebacks. I was tired of everything. I just wanted to go fall asleep somewhere for about seventy-two hours.

"Listen, I've had a tough day," I told him. "Is it okay if I go home now?"

"Yeah," he said. "Just tell me where I can reach you if I need you."

I gave him my home phone number and address. He wrote them down on a piece of paper. "Go ahead, get the hell out of my sight," he said.

I started to leave. But then I stopped, turned around, and stuck my head back in through the door.

"Hey, Lieutenant," I said, "I know you don't like me. But I just wanted to say that it's been a real pleasure working with you on this case. I think you're terrific. Honest."

He threw his pencil at me. "Get the hell out of here!" he bellowed. But I don't think he was really all that mad.

Outside Higgins was waiting for me.

"Want to get some coffee?" he asked.

"Why not?"

We drove to a Burger King. It was almost ten p.m., and the place was packed with screaming kids. We got two coffees at the counter and took them over to a table in the corner where the noise wasn't so bad.

"Jeez, it really was lucky I decided to follow you up here," Higgins said. "Otherwise, you might be a goner now."

"Yeah, lucky," I said.

"I checked with your office, you know. They told me where you went, and I just decided to take a ride up for the hell of it and see what you were up to. That's how I happened to be there, in case you were wondering."

I opened up a packet of sugar and poured it into my coffee.

"So tell me, Ed," I said quietly, "when did you start working for Tony Gianni?"

His head jerked in surprise. "What?"

"When did you start working for Gianni?"

He stared at me.

"So, that's what's bothering you. You've been acting funny all night. I figured you were just shook up. But now I see you've got something else on your mind."

"You haven't answered my question," I said.

"That's because it's too crazy to answer."

"It's not so crazy. You told me some things that no one but Gianni knew. And Gianni knew some things that I told you in private. It all adds up, Ed."

"You don't know what you're talking about."

"Don't I? The way I figure it you got to know him when you were in uniform in Bay Ridge a few years ago. It served his purpose to have someone on the police force working for him. When you were transferred to Narcotics, that was even better. Gianni does big business in narcotics. And now you're in Homicide. So Gianni knows everything the cops know about the Nancy Kimberly case. But then I come along and start uncovering some stuff that Gianni and the cops don't know about. So Gianni encourages you to romance me. Did he pay you to go out with me, Ed?"

"Now, wait a minute..."

"No, you wait a minute. It all paid off for him in the end, too, didn't it? I did find Nancy Kimberly when no one else—Gianni or the cops—could do it. But you were right behind me to get rid of her in a hurry. You killed her, which is what Gianni wanted all along. The mob boys—the ones he wanted to impress—will know he was behind the killing. And you did it all in the name of law and order."

I shook my head sadly.

"I should have known from the beginning by the way you lived," I said. "Not too many cops drive expensive cars like yours or live in big apartments or bet big money on games—all on their salary. You live high, Ed. Too high for an honest cop."

He ran his fingers through his hair.

"You going to go to Masters with this?"

"No, this has nothing to do with Masters. You can be a crooked cop for the rest of your life as far as I'm concerned. This is between you and me. It's about the end of our relationship."

"Would it make any difference if I told you I really care for you? I want to keep seeing you. I told them I wouldn't let them hurt you."

"No. No difference at all."

"Why not?"

"Look, let me try to explain something to you. I'm not the world's most honorable person by a long shot. But I do have a few basic principles I live by. Not many, but a few. So when Gianni offered me a lot of money to come work for him earlier today, I turned him down. You took the money. I could never live with that. Don't you see that?"

"I thought you really cared for me," he said. He reached toward me.

I pulled my hand away. "I did," I said.

"Well, I'm still the same person."

"No, that's where you're wrong," I told him. "The Ed Higgins I knew is dead. He died there on the front lawn along with Nancy Kimberly. Goodbye, Ed."

I walked out, got into my car and drove back to the city. Maybe if he had run after me and tried to get me to stop, I would have changed my mind. But he didn't. I never saw him again. Someone told me he quit the force later to work for a big private security firm up in Westchester, where he wound up marrying the boss's daughter. They've got one kid and are expecting another this year.

Some of the other people who were in my life then are gone too.

Dan Hodges had a heart attack and retired last year. His replacement: none other than your friend and mine, Annie Klein. It was a real surprise appointment, but it's worked out to be terrific. As for Barlow... well, he's still here. Somehow we manage to co-exist... but just barely.

Tom Donnelly? Well, I went to the barbecue at his house and we went out a couple more times after that. We got along pretty well. But there was really no place for that relationship to go. As the Nancy Kimberly case faded from the public eye, he started to lose interest. After a while he stopped calling. The last I heard he had gotten a big movie contract and moved to Hollywood. I read about him in the gossip rags.

Two-Ton Tony Gianni isn't around any more either—there's a new mob boss of bosses. About six months after the Kimberly killing, five ski-masked hoods carrying machine guns burst into Antonio's back room at lunch time. They opened fire on poor Tony right between the pasta and the steak pizzola. I covered his funeral. It was one of the biggest in New York City mob history.

As for the money—I don't think it was ever found. Nancy Kimberly seems to have taken that secret to the grave with her.

That's almost the end of the story. But not quite.

A few weeks after it all ended, a man and women came into the city room asking for me.

They were middle-aged, sun-tanned and well-dressed. Her hair was silver-blonde; he was tall and looked like a lawyer or a stockbroker.

"Miss Shannon?" the woman said. "We're the Kimberlys. Nancy's parents."

They had gotten back a few days before. They were still in a state of shock.

I asked them to sit down. I wasn't happy about this visit.

"She was our only child," Mrs Kimberly said.

"We're going to miss her very much," he said. "She was a beautiful girl."

"I don't know whether you have any children?" she said.

No, I said, I didn't.

"It seems just like yesterday I took Nancy home

from the hospital," her mother said. "It was June. She was born June 19, 1960. I remember it was a hot day. The car windows were open. She was wearing a little. . . a little bonnet. . ."

I squirmed in my chair.

"We came here to ask you a question," Mr Kimberly said. "I hope you don't mind."

"No, no. Can I get you some coffee?"

"No thanks." Mrs Kimberly was crying. Mr Kimberly said, "We've been reading the newspapers. But we don't believe those things. She was our daughter for twenty-three years. We know her better than anyone else. It's obscene, unthinkable, that Nancy would murder people—all those people, her boyfriend, the Langmann girl, the other girl. . ."

"You were with her at the end," Mrs Kimberly said. "She talked to you, you said so. Did she say she killed anyone? None of your articles said she confessed."

I looked at them. They probably were good people. They probably raised her the best way they knew how.

I stood up and faced them.

"It's true I was with her at the end," I said. "We talked for a long time. She told me she found the money and she never thought those men meant those threats. She didn't take it seriously until she found John Luckman's body. Then she rushed home and found Janet."

"Oh, poor Nancy," her mother said. "If only we had been home. She needed us."

"It was just one of those things," I said. "Don't blame yourself. If you were home, they might have killed all three of you."

That hit them.

"After all," I said, "they got rid of poor Karen Tunney."

"Those bastards," the father said. "Those bastards."

"They'll get theirs," I said. As it turned out, that was the only thing I said to them that was true.

"We should sue the police," Mr Kimberly said. "We should clear her name."

"Listen," I said quickly, "that would be a big mistake. They can do anything they want with the evidence, you know. Fingerprints, everything. I don't think Nancy would want you to spend your money and your time like that. I don't think the—" I swallowed. "—the poor kid would want the whole thing dragged out all over again."

"She's right," Mrs Kimberly said tearfully.

"And anyway," I said, "Gianni wouldn't like it."

That hit them again. I think it settled it.

We shook hands. Mrs Kimberly kissed me. They walked out feeling better. They should have. They were practically the only people close to Nancy Kimberly who were still alive.